I0570496

Coven of Desire

FANG

ELLEN MINT

Fang
ISBN # 978-1-83943-981-0
©Copyright Ellen Mint 2021
Cover Art by Erin Dameron-Hill ©Copyright May 2021
Interior text design by Claire Siemaszkiewicz
Totally Bound Publishing

FANG

Dedication

My endless gratitude to you, yes you, for picking up this book and reading it. For every book sold, my dog gets one treat…and she loves anyone who gives her treats.

Thank you to my all-mighty alpha reader Kristi, my word-whipping editor Rebecca, and my ARC team. This book would be a pile of American pudding without you.

Chapter One

A *crack* shattered the silence, trying to pry my locked jaws apart. Shadows clipped across the single floodlight above the floorboards.

Diesel, gun oil, salted pork and…old leather. Every scent filled my sinuses and I whimpered.

"Cal…"

No! I spun in the tight space, clamping my filthy fingers onto my brother's mouth. Even in the muddy crawlspace, I could see his eyes blazing above my palm. Eli's entire body shivered, his shoulders rising to shield himself from every clip of the boot above our heads.

"We have to keep moving," Mark spat in my ear. I cringed at the loogie sliding down my face while the eldest brother easily spun on his haunches. Even with his messed-up leg duct-taped to a fence post, he crawled quickly under the floor.

The boards above our heads stopped creaking and the light vanished. Had *he* gone to bed? This was it. Mom had put me in charge of getting Eli. All we had to do was…

Blinding white punctured the world. The ceiling above us shattered, splintering my heart. A massive hand slammed down right in front of my face. I reached my foot back, prepared to kick and break a finger, when the entire house collapsed over Eli.

Another crack. We all flinched as he took it. Three more lines added to the ones crisscrossing his back. Growls rumbled from Mark, pinned by his mother to stand and watch. I tried to twist away, but my head wouldn't leave. If I didn't watch, I could be next.

"Ah!"

A single cry escaped from Eli, and both Mark and I screamed, "No." If he made a sound, it started all over.

The belt hung against the five-year-old's back, Eli straining to reach over the apple crate he bent over. Crimson wicked up his burlap cassock. The blood would be left to dry for days as a reminder because the scars weren't enough.

"This is what happens to disobedient boys," boomed the voice through my ears, up my feet and into my blood. I tried to spit it out, the scent of him merging into a putrid taste boiling down my throat. Leaning over, I tried to retch it away—diesel, gun oil, salted pork, old leather, and blood. A spray of it erupted from my lips, staining the floorboards of the great room. No one turned to me, no one noticed I was vomiting in front of them.

Every eye gazed upon him. The father. Our great leader into the next stage of existence.

"Cal!"

"Eli…?"

His dirty, matted hair began to lift. As it did, crimson paint dribbled down the sides. "I don't wanna be here, Cal!"

"I..." Damn it. My gaze plummeted to the floor, tears threatening to burst. Slamming my lids closed so no one could tattle on me for crying, I said, "I'll get you out of here, Eli. When it's done, I'll get you."

"Forget it." It wasn't the soft cry of a kid, but the dead acceptance of an adult. Even with my eyes shut tight, I saw Eli rise from the box. He trampled it down with his foot, shattering the crate we'd all been whipped on. Eli stood tall, stretching far above my head.

"Weak," the voice of my unending nightmares thundered. "All of you." His face burned hot like the sun and I could only stare at the black gun extending from his hand. He pointed it at the followers standing in a ring around us.

"The time of the Moon is nigh," the rotten bastard said. "Destiny, child. Blood." He aimed his gun at Eli. A flash turned my brother's head into a wolf's skull.

"Eli!" I screamed, running for him. But my feet couldn't get any traction. Every step kept me pinned in place, unable to reach my brother slowly tumbling to the cement ground.

"You cannot escape it, Calvin." The asshole's hand clamped to my shoulder and he pressed me down to my knees. I tried to fight it, but my bones were matchsticks against his might. They buckled, my nose pressing into the dirt.

A wind howled through the trees, parting the stricken branches to reveal the yellow-blue light forever beaming down upon us. Itching rippled under my skin, one no amount of scratching would solve.

"Give in," he chanted almost serenely.

I shook my head, feeling fur and not hair brush against my shoulder. "No," I declared, the words warping as my gums receded. Pain clawed up the roots of my teeth sharpening to fangs.

"You cannot escape, Calvin."

Squeezing my eyes tight, I willed the wolf back. My teeth flattened. I patted my head, finding only the shaved hair. Lashing my arm back, I burst from his grip and took two steps forward. "I'm never changing again!" I shouted.

A low chuckle caused me to freeze. My body betrayed me, terror beckoning me to turn. Lucien bent down, half of his skull exposed, the skin ripped like paper, the muscles rotted away. The eyeball in his fleshless socket was milky white. "Child." A squishy, flapping sound followed his words. Red and purple tubes flapped out of a massive wound in his throat. I wanted to scream, but my mouth drowned with hot liquid.

"You cannot escape your blood."

Fuck!

I shook awake, my whole body slamming forward to try to escape. Instead of hurling myself off the bed, I almost knocked my teeth into a soft shoulder. Layla's hair provided cushioning to stop me, and I buried my face in it. I opened my mouth in a rictus and gave all the force of shrieking without letting a single sound escape.

My tongue tasted of copper and salt, of Lucien's blood that I had ripped from his throat. My brain thundered with the scents of his body, his boots, his instruments of terror. *Get out of it. He's not here. He can never be here.*

Burrowing my nose farther into her hair, I pulled in the deepest whiff imaginable. *Cereal marshmallows.* We'd gotten into a pointless food fight last night and I'd flicked them at her as she laughed. *Amber.* She'd used my soap to wash her hands and face. *Me.* The long night I held her safe in my arms. The air right before a thunderstorm struck. *Layla.*

My body tightened around her as it recognized the fullness of her. And she was stirring. Damn it.

"Cal…?" she croaked. Most of the time her voice was lush and lyrical, but in the morning it sounded more like a smoking frog.

I placed my lips to the nape of her neck, kissing over her curly hair to try to find the skin below. The taste of her replaced the lingering memory of blood. "Sorry to wake you," I said.

The wolf inside me was restless. *No, angry.* It wanted vengeance even though we'd already gotten it. I winced and started to slide away. If I stayed in bed, no matter how tempting, it could rip through me. *Take over my thoughts and push me to its side.* I slid my hand up Layla's stomach and over her hip, having to abandon her to calm down.

I was fairly certain she'd passed out and I slipped to my feet, when her fingers crested over mine. Through the shadows of the old house, I couldn't see much, but the silhouette of her breasts tumbling together out from under my blanket almost drove me back in with her.

"Are you okay?" she asked.

No. But I've never been okay my whole life. "You stay sleeping." I bent over and kissed her lips. I wished her taste and touch could chase away all the nightmare, but it clung to me like a filthy sack caked in blood. Rising to my feet, I stumbled out of my room. The wolf inside me howled.

Chapter Two

Ice-cold water splattered the back of my hand. Rather than step back and wait for the old house's pipes to warm, I faced the freezing shower head-on. My skin prickled in goosebumps, the water like shards stabbing into my pores. A low growl rumbled from deep in my chest, the wolf wanting out.

I slapped both hands to the shower tile and dunked the back of my head into the stream. All I could stare at were my grubby toes shuffling under the water. I'd been in the basement last night. An hour as the wolf was all I needed to work it out of my system.

Why was the water so cold still? Sure, the house was ancient, a damn near gift from another in the werewolf underground — which was less sexy twenty-somethings in tight leather pants and more an unlisted discord group for werewolves. They'd post about safe spots to change, holes to hide clothing in, hotels friendly to "pets" and discounts on flea and tick sprays. There was nothing alluring about this life, the dirt trapped under my nails from when they'd been claws telling the story.

Over a month ago, I'd killed the asshole who had shot my brother. Who'd abused and tortured us until we escaped as kids. Who was my father.

Should I feel elated? My brothers and I had lived in unending fear that one day he'd find us, drag us back to his compound and we'd never be free again. But no more. *He's dead.*

I wrung a hand over my chin, frowning at the rising stubble. A pain lingered in the back of my jaw that usually vanished after I transformed out of the wolf.

"It's stress," I whispered to myself. The old pipes groaned, slowing the water pressure to a drip, but finally the shower turned warm...then scalding. I twisted the knob, not shifting out of the spray even as my ears burned. They'd probably look funny so bright red against my white-blond hair.

I hated it. One summer, I'd spent every day I could in the cheap-ass city pool, hoping the green tint would be permanent. To finally rip away that mark. We were all stuck with the same eyes, but his hair...

Stop thinking about him. He's dead. The cult's...who the fuck cares. They'd gone silent as Thanksgiving became Christmas. I'd tried to keep an eye on the compound, but the sudden downfall of snow made trudging to the woods treacherous—far too easy for guards to track a man or beast in that weather.

The light shifted. I yanked my head from the downpour and was about to spin around when chilled hands cupped around my chest. She pressed her cheek flush with my back, and my rapid heartbeat calmed itself.

"I thought you might like some company," Layla said, most of the croak gone out of her voice.

Her company was the only thing I wanted anymore. Work. School. Tests. Transformation. Eating. Sleeping—there was no joy to be found in any aspect of my life…except for Layla.

I caught her fingers wafting through my soaked chest hair and pulled them to my lips to kiss her knuckles. Her body caressed against mine, her breasts molding to my back. How I wanted to take both in my palms and tug on her nips until she squeaked. The tuft of her pubic hair grazed my ass and a moan slipped free.

The wolf knew her body's reactions. It smelled the flush of her skin dewing in arousal. It heard her heartbeat picking up in tempo, the micro-gasps that made no sound to the human ear.

I spun so fast water beads whipped off in all directions. A groggy smile clung to her lips, the humid shower highlighting the petal-pink color against the tawny hue of her skin. Dew drops beaded across her entire body that kicked off a pant in my throat. But it was her eyes that ensnared me, wide in her face and so round they almost looked like perfect spheres. I was entranced with them, with the deep brown color that bore a trace of green in the bright summer light and her dark lashes that brushed to the sides naturally like curtains before a work of art.

"You're so damn…" I said, but the words in my throat garbled to a growl. I dove for her lips while focusing on her eyes. The jolt of surprise in her irises was eclipsed by hunger, the slow flutter of her lids slipping closed as she folded her hands around my neck and tugged me closer.

Every lingering taste from my dream vanished, my mouth flooding with only Layla. I pressed her pillowy lips open and plunged my tongue inside, needing more of her. All of her. She tugged on my hair, guiding me to kiss her harder than before.

Nip her. Scrape your teeth down her throat. Bite right at the top of her breast until she squeals in delight.

My hand cupped to her neck, causing Layla to break off the kiss. Those wide, beautiful eyes hooded and she turned her jaw to the side. An invitation.

Yes. Bite her. She'll cream from it.

Running my nose against the hollow behind her ear and down, I trailed my lips to her throat…and placed a soft kiss instead. Layla giggled in delight, while the wolf inside me pouted. It'd had enough attention already.

Cupping my hands to the side of her face, I scattered the water droplets on her forehead with my thumbs. "How can you be so beautiful the second you wake up?"

She snorted at that. "You are a terrible liar."

"No. I'm painfully…" I swept my palms over her breasts, my body jerking at the moan slipping from her lips. "Awkwardly…" My hips twitched, the need to thrust sending my cock pulsing into her belly. *Fuck.* Stars shattered in my eyes, telling me this wasn't going to be a slow and gentle session.

Layla tossed her head back, her spirals of hair flattening against the shower tile. Another moan from her kicked off one in me.

I dove to her lips, about to press a kiss when I whispered, "Honest."

She began to snicker at the truth, but I cut her off with a kiss. With one hand, I kept tugging on her nipple straining to its full peak even in the warmth of the shower. The other hand I swept down the side of her waist to the demanding throb between my legs. One squeeze was usually enough to calm it and give me more time, but Layla caught my wrist…and rolled her palm right over the crown of my cock.

"Fu-uck!" My teeth chattered at the pulse of pleasure striking through me.

Her smile brightened as she released her grip on me. Layla dug her fingers into my hips, twisting me until the shower splattered onto my back. *What is she…?*

When she started to descend to a knee, a dumbstruck guffaw rose in my throat. *Be cool.* I managed to swallow the laugh down even while my libido fired up in joy. Rubbing into her shoulder for support, I wasn't certain what to do with my other hand.

On her head? No. The other shoulder? That could be bad. What if I just…? Folding my fingers back, I caressed the knuckles against her cheek. They curled back as she opened her mouth wide and sucked the tip of me in.

Holy shit! She twirled her tongue around me like a slick ribbon. The pressure started softly, but increased as she pulled more of me into her mouth. Oh, fuck! Tightening her lips, Layla pressed them into my shaft while the back of her tongue rumbled over the crown.

My toes clenched in the lukewarm water splashing under my feet. I tried to get a grip, to calm the rampaging blood coursing straight to my crotch. Then she worked my balls first with a gentle roll of them in her palm. She parted down my scrotum and pressed her thumb, behind…

Water dribbled down my cheek, causing me to glance down. To the beautiful woman sucking me off, her perfect tits glistening in dew.

Point of no return! I tried to push on Layla's cheek, to warn her what was coming, but she increased her stroking and hung on. "God damn it all," I sputtered, the orgasm striking through me. I reveled in my cum racing through my cock, expanding it until Layla's teeth grazed the skin.

Fucking hell! That was even better. An incoherent cry slipped past me and my body shivered in joy. I didn't want to move, certain that if I opened my eyes the pleasure would vanish.

A chill crested against the tip of my slathered cock and my paradise was shattered. But Layla's sweet smile and her brushing her palms over my butt, the small of my back, and up to my shoulders brought me back home. She bit her lip and worked her jaw from the strain.

"Well…?" she asked, and hopped up on the balls of her feet before landing back down. "How's that for a wakeup call?"

A giddy laugh rolled in my lungs. Brushing back her fallen hair, I said, "You're better than coffee."

She twisted her lips, flattening the top one in a crooked smile. But I wanted to feel them in their full rounded glory. Taking her in a kiss, I pulled her chest to mine and reveled in her soft breasts pooling against my ropey muscles and her rounded thighs molding over my strong ones.

Making Layla whimper and moan, hearing her beg for me to never stop, was the only reason I woke from my slumber. I needed her more than ever.

"I want you," I growled, my words crackling in urgency.

She tipped her chin. "I hadn't planned on going anywhere. You don't have another shower."

"No." I shook my head, my skin prickling with impatience. "I want you to scream in pleasure."

Her eyes widened in surprise for a flicker, but there was that circle of hunger. The one I'd stoke every time she was in my arms. She kissed me, hard, the strength of her lips that'd sucked me off instantly controlling mine. Layla shifted her chin, as if she was trying to knock her hair away, but I was lost in caressing her ass and she was too busy hanging on to me. Maybe I could...

A hand swept over her jaw, scattering her soggy hair back. "Allow me," the demon whispered.

For a moment, Layla leaned back into him, her eyes shut tight as the demon pressed a kiss to her lips wet from my tongue. Her lids snapped open and she shivered out of his grip. "*Ink?* What are you doing here?"

He didn't answer, only held out his hands to his completely naked body. I snaked my fingers back and kept my eye line level with the top of the shower.

"This isn't funny," Layla berated the demon bound to her, the incubus she'd agreed to feed.

"Am I chortling? Guffawing? Have I split open my sides in laughter?"

I shuddered. That was my cue to leave. "Excuse me," I said, tugging back the shower curtain beside the spray. Water beaded over the floor, but I didn't care about possible mold damage at the moment.

"Cal, wait..." Layla tried to reach for me, but I slipped away and wrapped a towel around my waist. She moved to take a step out, when I glanced to her.

"Stay," I said. "Wash up. I'll..." My lips fumbled with a smile. "Go make breakfast."

With that, I left Layla and her pet demon to bicker in the shower together.

Chapter Three

The second it popped free, I crammed the half-burnt toast into my mouth. Rather than chew it to pieces, I cracked an egg into my skillet, watching the translucent whites bubble up and shift in the heat. Even over the hiss of the pan, I could hear the groan of my pipes. They weren't happy about having to send all that hot water up to my shower.

After giving the pan a quick shake of, I tossed the egg into the air and caught it. No one waited in the kitchen, impressed by my skill. Which was probably good as a chunk of the whites tumbled off the edge of the pan and incinerated in the burner. Layla in her little tank top and shorts...no. In my shirt, the one so old she didn't even need to be wet for it to cling to her breasts, revealing nearly the entire outline of them.

We could sit at the breakfast nook with light streaming through the window and little robins chirping from the garden, one daring enough to draw close to the sill. She'd try to coax it in, offering crumbs of bread until the brave little bird hopped into her hand.

Stupid. My kitchen was a tiny square of diabolical torture. There was barely any room for me to cook, never mind an alcove for a little table to bask in dawn's light.

I bit off a corner of my toast, the bread dissolving down my throat. Plates were too much work, so I shook the egg on top of my remaining toast and leaned against the counter eating both. Absently, I tugged my phone off its charger and began to scroll through whatever I'd missed last night.

My eyes darted to the last message from Mark. It didn't say much. Certainly not where he was, or where he was heading. Only a short note telling me that he'd got out fine, and I wouldn't hear from him for a long time.

He'd taken the blame, all of it. Not just for having murdered our father, but for losing Eli too. *Setting off a potential pack war that hadn't been seen in decades.* Yet, none of that bothered him. That last night, Mark had seemed almost excited about facing off against the cult and anyone else in league with them, giddy to be free to fight back after years of being trapped under the alpha's thumb.

No goodbyes. No mention of regrets. Not even a wish for hope. All he'd left me with was a single order. "Don't fall for the witch."

"What is that smell?"

A headache jabbed between my eyebrows. Instead of a beautiful woman draped in a sopping towel, I stared at the incubus. He wore his usual outfit of a red shirt and black pants, though his hair was drenched to his head as if he hadn't even paused to dry off before dressing. He darted his inhuman, flame-colored eyes down my body.

I'd never felt unnerved by being naked around other men—it was hard to bring clothes with me when in wolf form. But the way the demon stared made me glad I'd slipped on my flannel pajama bottoms at least.

"I'm making eggs," I said, chewing up the last of my breakfast and meeting him eye to eye.

He scratched his chin, the sound of sandpaper erupting from his unnatural stubble, and crinkled his nose. "Those come from a chicken's anus. Where is that box of delightful bear-based crunch puffs?" Ink pushed past me, caring nothing for the fact that he was in my home, and dug into the pantry.

Little more than a closet beside the stove, my pantry was crammed to bursting to feed me. I'd stocked up on a few of Layla's favorite foods for when I needed her to stay over. I hadn't counted on the demon tailing along.

The demon who came as part of the bargain in this couple shoved his head in my cabinets. What he was unsettled me, to say the least. An incubus, a creature of lust. They fed off not sugary cereals but sex, and he was bound to Layla until she learned enough magic to get rid of him.

He'd been haunting her, so to speak, for over two months and she seemed okay. But I couldn't shake the feeling that the demon was hiding something and one day he might stop playing gentle with her.

"There they are. Golden treasures of morning," Ink cried as he hefted out a box of kid's cereal.

"I'll get you a..." When I reached for a bowl, he opened the top, raised it to his mouth and dumped a spray of yellow cereal puffs in. "Never mind."

Crackling and crunching sounds were all that filled the silence. I tried to not stare in abject horror at the demon stuffing his face to the brim, but it was hard to look away. When he reached for a snack cake to add to the mass of sugar, I finally twisted to my windows.

Where was Layla? I'd only left them maybe five minutes ago. That didn't speak well for the demon designed for sex. "You must eat as rapidly as you…*eat*."

"Come again?"

I abandoned my vigil and turned to find the incubus with his cheeks bulging. He didn't look imposing, the chipmunk of a man dripping in my kitchen. "It's nice to know that you can only last a few minutes before you have to roll off her."

"Oh! This is that…that human thing. Do we beat chests? I've always wanted to try that. Though it tends to end in me ripping off someone's doublet with my teeth." The demon laughed and began to squeeze the water off his hair, letting the excess puddle on the floor. "If you must know, after you left I received nothing more than a tongue lashing. Not the one you got, sadly. And our dear Layla chose to bathe alone."

What? "Aren't you here to…to feed or whatever it is you do?"

A laugh cracked his face. Even with me knowing he was a demon, my nose curdling at the stench of brimstone on him, my eyes couldn't deny how unfairly handsome he was. Full on jeering at me while standing in a puddle in his socks, he looked like he could advertise suits.

"I'm here because Layla desired me to be."

A frown built up across my face. She'd swung by late last night after her shift, after I'd finished transforming, and I'd held her in my arms until we both passed out. There had been no time for her to contact him. "When?" I scoffed.

Ink tipped his head in thought, "Let's see. She'd swallowed the last of your semen, rose to her feet and wished for me to arrive."

He's lying. My fists bunched and my heart thundered. *That smug fucking face, he's lying to screw with me. Why? Because he's a demon. That's what they do. Lie and fuck.*

"Oh god, are you cooking?"

I pivoted around at her voice, my hands falling open. Shit. Blood weeped from my palms. The demon had pissed me off so much that my nails had transformed into claws, and I hadn't even noticed. Clamping my hands to my thighs, I turned to Layla and smiled.

"I was... Is that a problem?"

"Only in that I missed it," she said, gliding across the floor and wrapping a hand around my shoulder. I kept my palms on my pants, trying to soak up the blood so she wouldn't notice. A frown crossed her lips, and instead of kissing me, she pecked me on the cheek instead.

Layla struggled to push past the demon in the room. While she fished for one of the protein bars, she cupped his arm and he brazenly rested his palm on her ass. A cough escaped my teeth. Before they could all turn in judgment on me, I said, "This kitchen is too...tiny."

It was one of a dozen thoughts stampeding through my head for attention, and the least likely to cause all-out war. Layla's gaze darted from me shrinking in on myself to the smirking demon. "Do you have to be here?" she prompted Ink.

He grinned wider and shook his head. "Not at all. Do I wish to be...?" Tipping his chin down, he leaned closer until his lips almost grazed Layla's ear. "Also no."

That declaration sent her twisting to the demon. Ink caught her cheek in his hand and kissed her. Heat crackled up my stomach and I glared at the floor.

"Until you call me again, my bond," the demon declared. He gave one last kiss to Layla's parted lips and vanished. There was no *poof* of air, no smoke. Not even a handful of glitter. He was simply there crammed halfway into my pantry one second, then gone the next. I could still smell him though.

Layla rubbed her lips as if she was trying to remove his touch, or seal it in. "He's…um…"

Bound to her. An aspect in her life that was as immutable as my claws. I knew that. I accepted that fact. So why did it feel awkward whenever the incubus stormed in without a second's thought?

She must have felt the same, her apology fading as her cute nose wrinkled at the top. The consternation grew, Layla bunching her fingers together and the furrows spidering across the sides of her eyes. Without pause, I swept her up in my arms and kissed the bridge of her nose.

A deep breath escaped from Layla, and I tried to pretend I was releasing my stress at the same time. "Are you…doing okay?" she asked me.

"Why?" I began, wanting to laugh. Kissing first the apple of her cheek, I began to loop my way down to her lips. Hooking my thumb under her chin, I tugged her head up and paused. Her mouth was beautiful, the tempting lips parted so a hint of her front teeth and the delicate gap emerged. But a whiff of brimstone lingered where he'd been.

Layla cupped my wrist, worrying her palm back and forth in a circle. "You were tossing a lot last night," she said, eyes shimmering in concern.

The thought made me smile with all the bitter sweetness I could. Not caring who'd been there before, I kissed her deeply and purely. The heat of her soul tingled through me, beckoning me for more. *The demon's gone, and there is an empty kitchen table just down the hall.*

What if she calls to him again? Desires him?

Breaking off the kiss, I knotted back on my *everything's fine* smile. "It happens, especially the closer a full moon gets." I pecked the rounded tip of her nose and stepped back. Fishing my coffee cup from below the slow drip, I winced at the lukewarm brew but drank it anyway.

"Cal, are you sure there isn't something you want to talk about?"

The wince pulled clear down my throat, wrenching my shoulder. "Shit, warn a guy before you pull out the 'we need to talk' card."

She folded her arms across her chest, but the edges of her pursed lips lifted. Layla knew I was kidding. "Give me some credit. I only do that when it's two in the morning and we have to work the next day."

"Good to know I have no chance of winning any argument with you." Tucking the mug to my stomach in the hope my blush would re-heat it, I scrolled through my phone. There wasn't anything I wanted to find, but the action numbed my brain.

"I'm just...I'm worried."

"About what?" *Huh. A new email. How much money can I make at home thanks to this one housewife that doctors hate?*

"You," Layla said, her tone growing sharper. My ears tingled, telling me to look up, when I spotted who'd sent me the email. "You were talking in your sleep last night. About Eli."

"Oh fuck," my brain and tongue sputtered at the same time. My face must have turned paper white as Layla leaned closer and tried to peer down at my phone. But I held it tight to my eyes, hoping I'd misread the email from my mother.

Fuck!

"What?"

This wasn't supposed to happen so soon! My body dashed about in the kitchen, tossing plates and cups either into the sink or onto the counter. It moved without input from my brain because my mind kept screaming in confusion.

"Cal!" A force surged up my legs, sticking them to the ground. I glared at the witch waving her fingers through the air, the spell lingering on her lips. At my accusing look, Layla tipped her head to the floor. "You dropped a glass and shattered it."

I hadn't even heard that happen.

She waved her fingers and the force holding me in place evaporated. I stumbled away from the glass shards I'd nearly stepped on. Layla hustled over with the dustpan and started to clean up the mess while I stared in disbelief. *How didn't I notice?*

"What is it? What's wrong? Is it Mark?"

"Yes. No. It's... I've been summoned by my mother."

A look of confusion and exhaustion crossed Layla's face. She didn't understand. I barely did.

"A pack knows Lucien is dead. And if they aren't satisfied that it was done in self-defense...they could kill my mom."

Layla shot up to her feet. She nearly walked on the glass to reach me, but I picked her up in my arms. How could they already have known? The cult was in disarray, and hunting for a leader. Calls of revenge weren't put out until a new alpha could make them. What was going on?

"I have to get to Santa Fe. I have to…to talk to them. Set this all right. Convince them that Mark—" *That Mark killed my father. A lie I must keep alive or it could kill my only remaining brother.*

"Cal?"

A warm hand pressed to my frozen cheek, shocking me out of my state. I stared in confusion to find I'd carried her to the front door. Snow tumbled inside, freezing my bare feet solid. I'd almost thrown her out into the literal cold in her pajamas without a second thought.

Regret burned on my face. I gazed down, hoping she couldn't see my eyes. "I'll let you get dressed," I said, dropping her to her feet away from the snow. "While I try to book a flight to New Mexico."

"I can help," Layla responded. She'd reached for the banister, but paused with one foot on the stair to watch me.

What help could she give? If the pack didn't believe me, there was a high chance they'd turn on her. If they didn't even care for the truth and only wanted vengeance, it'd be a bloodbath, no matter what. With a forced smile, I said, "I know," and began to hunt for flights to the southwest.

Chapter Four

Come the fuck on!

I cranked my keys forward, praying for anything but the *ung-ung-ung* noise to sputter from the engine. *Damn it!* Why was this so hard? I couldn't book a flight because every seat was crammed with people returning from their holiday vacations. *And what did I do for Christmas? Spent half the day restocking while a broken loop of* Jingle Bells *twisted from the speakers like a wraith sent from hell to drive me mad.* Even if I had the two grand I needed to book a flight to Santa Fe last minute, there wasn't a standing plank they could strap my body to.

Of course, right when I needed to start a twenty-hour drive, my truck decided to give up on life. *Ahh!* I slammed my palm into the wheel, setting off the wheezing horn. It blasted through the snow-draped morning, startling my neighbor in the middle of scooping her drive.

Fuck. I stumbled out of the frostbitten cab and worked the hood open. I was supposed to be on the road by now. With no stops, I could beat the advancing pack by a day and a half. What was I supposed to do now?

Absently, I tugged on the radiator cap, inspected the dipstick and bunched my fists tighter together. I knew what was wrong. It was the fucking starter. *Again.* I didn't have time to get a part, much less replace it. Not that it'd last long in this weather. Every winter the damn thing died. My truck missed the desert more than I did.

Sand in my paws, the horizon a velvet blanket coated in glitter. I'd run with the coyotes, my howl echoing off the gnarled mountains and rocks rising from the red land. It felt like heaven compared to the freezing snow and press of people always posting on NosyNeighbor about that "big dog running through the yards".

How was I going to get back with no truck before the shit really hit the fan?

After wiping off the battery connections, in the foolish hope it might be that, I tugged open the driver door and reached in to try again. My ears perked up. If I'd been in wolf form, they'd have fully swiveled around at the sound of a small sedan careening through the snow. A lightness wrapped around my heart and my foot tapped in excitement.

Damn it. No. This doesn't concern her.

I'd gotten another round of absolutely nothing from my truck by the time the car stopped behind me. Her shoes crinkled in the snowy tire ruts on the street, setting off the wolf inside. But as I accepted defeat and turned to face her, my heart stuck in my throat.

She stood out like a snow fairy against the whitewashed background, the tip of her round nose almost as red as Rudolph's. Her skin glowed, setting her apart from the bland sky and street. The darker freckles against her light brown looked like little elf marks where magic kissed her across the cheek.

"I was afraid I missed you," Layla called and scampered across the road to my side. "This storm's a beast."

All the impotent rage from my stranded truck evaporated. I curled her in my arms and kissed her. She smelled of cinnamon and nutmeg, exactly like those cookies that Fariah had sent us. I thought Layla had already eaten her stash. *Did she take one of mine?*

I wanted to call her out on it, turn it into a game that'd send us both running for my kitchen or the bedroom. But she stared at my truck with its innards exposed to the elements, and frowned. "Not going so well?"

My happy little illusion plunged into a snowbank. I couldn't play house with her because I was needed halfway across the country. Even if I did, her demon would pop in just as I was about to... *Never mind.*

"I don't know what to do. No flights. My truck's DOA. I guess I could try to rent a car, if you wouldn't mind dropping me off?" An overwhelming urge to tip my head back and scream reverberated through me. Instead, I folded my fingers up tightly and tried to squeeze it away. Pain caught along the scab on my palm, but I shook it off.

Layla glanced back to her car, probably trying to figure out how to clean it so I could fit in. We both shared that living-in-our-vehicles trait which caused fast food bags to spontaneously appear in wheel wells. "What if we take my car?"

"To the rental place?" That was what I'd hoped, though I could call a car if she had somewhere else to be.

She brushed her palm over my cheek, tracing her thumb against my bottom lip. "No. To Santa Fe."

"That's not..." I couldn't. Not after everything that happened with Mark. And Eli. Layla was already at the passenger side, pulling out a wad of trash from the seat. "I don't think that's a good idea."

"Why not? My car can handle it, better than your truck. Even if we got it started now, what are the chances you wouldn't be stranded on the interstate?"

Less than ideal. I gritted my teeth, glaring at my diesel traitor.

"Or are you worried after a couple hours stuck together in the car, we'll hate each other so much we end the whole thing?"

"No! Not at... You're joking."

She shrugged as if that wasn't her greatest concern, but it was still a possibility. A test of our relationship wasn't high on my problem list. But Layla started to shrink and I had to unravel my tongue and explain.

"The pack is, it's dangerous. If I don't explain myself—"

"They'll kill you," she interrupted, her eyes cracking in pain.

I couldn't stand the sight and pulled her flushed forehead to my frozen one. "They'll kill anyone in their way."

"So I should come. You know, be back up. In case you forgot..." She twisted her fingers around and flicked them. A spark of fire cracked off. It wasn't much, but it did make me smile. She'd been working on that spell for weeks.

Yes, she was a witch. Yes, she had magic. But if I let her get hurt, if she was injured or worse because of my life...? I'd already buried one brother in the soggy ground. I couldn't handle leaving her in the sand. Layla stared at me, waiting for an explanation or acceptance.

Unable to give either, I said, "Werewolves aren't exactly fans of witches either."

"That's because they haven't met me yet. I happen to be quite nice when I want to be."

I snickered and tugged her closer so my lips grazed her forehead. But Layla wasn't easily swayed by a little affection. "Cal, I...I have no idea what this werewolf pack shit is about. But I want to, I need to help you. I can be another witness to back up that you had every right to kill—"

My arms tightened around her on instinct, cutting off the truth masquerading as a lie. Layla caught on quickly, and amended, "That your brother had every right to kill the asshole."

The more we said that even with no other ear around, the easier it was to believe. I brushed back her hair, letting the single pink strand tumble through my fingers. "It's not like that. I... Werewolf justice isn't American justice."

"American justice isn't justice," Layla said quickly under her breath. "Look, I'd...I'd feel much better if I came with you. And we could tag team on driving. Give you a chance to sleep in the car?"

I shouldn't let her do this. If she stayed here, she'd be safe. No pack questioning the seeming human at my side. No chance of her walking into the middle of a full-on fang fight and getting hurt. No risk of my mother asking why I was dating a witch with a demon for a pet.

I knew in my heart that going alone was best for everyone involved.

"Okay," I said, my lips twisting into a smile. "Let's go together."

My heart wasn't strong enough to disappoint her.

Chapter Five

Ten miles to the state border. The hypnotic *thunk* of the wheels spinning at seventy miles an hour percolated through the car. I kept glancing over at Layla, who had spent the last half hour with both her hands on the wheel and eyes straight ahead.

Without thought, I started to reach for the radio, hoping music would cut through the awkward silence. But a larger gulf rose before me. What would she want to listen to? Did she even want music on while driving? Maybe she was more of a book-on-tape person.

Her gaze darted from the highway cutting through snow-dampened cornfields to me. As a smile rose on her lips, sweat dripped down my back. My mouth opened and the dumbest possible thing escaped. "I spy with my little eye..."

Layla snickered. "You can't be serious."

Wrinkling my nose, I leaned back into the bucket seat. Pain lanced up my side from a crick. I didn't realize I'd been on the actual edge to the point of causing a cramp. "No, not really." One hour down, twenty-one to go. This was going to be a long car ride.

"Can I ask about this werewolf justice and what it all entails?"

A shrug tried to roll off my shoulder, but the cramp increased. Instead, I dug my fingers into the muscle and said, "I won't stop you, but I barely understand it. We've been living outside of the whole system since…" My jaw slammed shut, the lifetime of lying about my past taking control. The air grew heavier with my unspoken words, and I had to get them out. "Since escaping the cult," I added, watching the stripe of rumble bars on the side of the highway.

"All you have to do is prove to these other werewolves that the asshole was a threat?" Layla asked. An ironic laugh rumbled in my mind at even her avoiding my father's name. We'd never used it as kids, always falling back on *asshole* or *bastard* if we had to mention him at all. I guess some habits were so hard to break that they just infected others.

The hairs on the back of my neck rose, telling me I was being watched. I caught her brown-eyed gaze flitting to me, wanting an answer. The *sorry* hung on my tongue, and I rubbed a hand over my face. "Not…not quite."

"What? Do you need the gun? Please don't tell me they won't believe you without a body."

I didn't ask if she meant Eli's or the asshole's. Not that it mattered. We certainly didn't have either in the car. Pain socked into the back of my head at the cold idea of Eli's wide frame folded up and tossed inside a dark trunk. But I'd left him in the dark, without even a stone to mark his resting place.

"They don't care that the" —I sucked in a breath and forced out—"that Lucien murdered Eli."

"What? Why not?"

This was the part I hated having to explain, hated having to think about. "Because, as far as the other packs are concerned, Lucien could do whatever he wanted to Eli. To Mark. To me. He was the alpha, so he owned us."

"Fucking hell," Layla spat. "What the shit is wrong with them?"

I wanted to shrug it away, maybe claim that it was all part of werewolf tradition, but venom twisted in my soul. The truth was that just as many werewolves refused to be a part of a pack like that. They survived just fine, people who'd gotten out or weren't even born in them. They formed families. Lived happy lives away from the structure they told us we'd die without.

More than just werewolves were in the cult, but the wolves ran the show. And every day they told us, reminded us that without the pack, without the alpha keeping us in check, we'd lose our minds. Abandon walking on two-legs, escape into the forest and turn fully feral. We could only count on each other for safety.

It was all bullshit, but bullshit I couldn't stop worrying about late at night while sleeping alone and unaccounted for.

"But you escaped the cult, pack, whatever bullshit name they invented to excuse their abuse!" Layla's thunder brought a smile to me. I was so tired of being angry at it all, at the reason why we ran and hid from the people like us. But I also knew I couldn't stop being angry either, or I might fall back into the lies they wove into my brain from the crib.

"Not really. Far as the other packs are concerned, you're in it for life unless the alpha dismisses you."

"I'm guessing that doesn't mean he sends you out with a handful of gift cards and a fruit basket."

My only answer was a solitary harsh laugh. What was a pack even doing in New Mexico? Mom had taken us farther and farther south because almost all the American ones kept to the north. Did they go after her on purpose? Or was one expanding its territory and hoping to take an alpha's?

"Is this all a kangaroo court then?" Layla asked, causing me to frown in confusion. "They already decided you're guilty because you're not a free person. Jesus Christ, that is fucked up. No one is owned, not by their parents or anyone else."

She said it so fervidly it felt like a quote, or hard-fought mantra. And, despite us having been friends for over a year and a half, it hit me how little I knew of her past…because I didn't want to tell her of mine either.

All in good time. Maybe later today since we were trapped in the car together, if she was up for it. I noticed her clenched jaw and mine responded in kind. The same ache from when I'd transform.

"It's possible I could be cleared. There are reasons for someone to challenge the alpha."

"Like if he's an abusive asshole?" she said in a mocking tone. We both knew the chances of that one holding up against another pack's inquiry.

The truth was that my only saving grace could be the reason I hated looking in a mirror most days. "A child of the alpha can challenge them for control," I whispered, darting my gaze anywhere but her.

"Cal…" The hand she'd had gripped to the wheel broke off and Layla cupped my knee. "Whatever happens, I'll be there to shoot lightning at wolves for you."

A kind thought. But I doubted her magic could do much against the full might of a pack seeking justice. They weren't doing this out of some sort of sympathy for Lucien or the Endless Moon. No, it was as much a power grab as a reminder to other wolves that they must obey the alpha or suffer consequences. There was a good chance they already decided I was to be an example and no witch could stop that.

Rather than worry Layla, I brushed my hand to her cheek. "Thank you," I said.

Her bright eyes held mine a beat, before darting to the green signs. "We're about to pass mile marker zero. Hold your breath," she said. I'd never heard of such a tradition, but took a deep breath and slammed my mouth shut.

Both our cheeks bulged, Layla looking like an adorable chipmunk as we fought to keep the air in. I caught the next mile marker in the distance, a blue one with the number three hundred and seventy-something on it. Without thought, I reached over to catch Layla's hand. Our fingers entwined together, our breath held as we crossed into a new state and whatever danger lay ahead.

"Where are we heading?"

The voice shot through the car like a cannon. Layla's lips burst apart, her held breath escaping as an "Oh fuck!" The car jerked wildly to the side, half the tires striking the rumble bars and bouncing us in our seats. "Ink!" she screamed, twisting the wheel under her to get us back onto the interstate.

Horns blared in all directions, people either terrified or judgmental of the car that had taken a little detour to the side of the road. I tried to glance around, certain I'd find a raised finger or two in our direction. Layla clamped her hands to the wheel and whipped her head over her shoulder.

"What are you doing here?" she screamed.

The incubus sat dead center in the backseat, his straddling legs in both wheel wells and a grand smile on his face. Without a care, he pivoted his head from me back to Layla who looked about to leap out of the driver's seat to strangle him. With a chuckle, Ink said, "That's what I want to know…my bond."

"I will fucking bond *you*," Layla spat.

Honking increased, this time at the car slowing to a crawl on the interstate. "Um, babe," I said, about to reach over and take the wheel myself. A snarl raising her lips, Layla snaked a hand back to try to grab Ink's collar, or throat. But she shook the attack off and turned to face the road ahead.

Obviously having the time of his life, Ink rested both elbows on the sides of the headrests and leaned forward. The edge of his hair slicked against my cheek, causing me to sit bolt upright. I felt his eyes dart to me, but it couldn't have been for long as he turned to fully face Layla, who looked like she was weighing the idea of opening the door and tossing him out. I could certainly give a push should the need arise.

"I thought I left you in the apartment. You were watching your usual round of court TV and infomercials." It sounded like she said that less to Ink and more for me. I'd been sitting in the car while she'd dashed to her apartment to pack. It hadn't been for long, though I was surprised when she'd rushed out alone. *So much for that single glimmer of hope.*

"Yes. About a hose that fits inside one's pocket...which I imagine could cause a pinching sensation to the hose already inside the pants."

"Ink..." she snarled, so fully exasperated that I snickered. My memory slipped back to Layla, in the middle of a study session, blowing a sigh so hard it sent her notes flying into the high winds. We never did get the ones on thrombosis back.

But she had no idea I was remembering her being adorable and her anger cut through me instead. Shutting up, I waved my hands in the air and turned to face the landscape. There sure was a lot of interesting brown grass out there.

"Congratulations," the demon said, "you've discovered the exact distance which the bond can be stretched."

Only the thud of the tires burst through the car, and I caught Layla returning the same look. *What?*

"I'd thought it much shorter. The length an ox can pull a cart in a day, but apparently not. That was the point of this experiment, no?"

"Are you telling me, that because of this...soul bond thing—?"

"Not a soul bond as I am happily devoid of a soul."

Fighting through his forest of dark hair, I turned to Ink. "You are always with her?" My soul plummeted as my brain took in what I said. There was literally no escaping the incubus, not even for a day. He'd be there no matter what, no matter how far we ran.

The demon chuckled. "I am always aware of her and her desires regardless of distance. But physically, yes. We cannot be separated by...how many oxen pulls is it?"

"What if I pulled over right now and left you on the side of the road?" Layla asked. Her voice sounded flustered, her heartbeat increasing erratically. Was she feeling trapped by the thought too?

Ink shrugged. "I'd stand in place watching the world go by until the tether snapped me back to your side. Did I not mention this before?"

"No, you fucking well..." Layla began, wringing her fingers through the air. "So I'm stuck with you?"

"Until you release me, or the world ends. Whichever comes first. I am surprised at *your* surprise, however. Did you really think I'd let you face off against an entire werewolf pack without me?"

I wasn't going to let her, no matter what. Even them knowing a witch was around could set off an attack. But Layla might have ignored me, or tried to help any way. God help me, but I found myself glad Ink had invited himself on this trip.

"Cal...?" Layla swiveled her head. I wished I could read her thoughts as easily as her pet demon did. Her lips were pursed tight as if she wanted to spit venom from them, but her eyes were wary and rueful. "What do you think? It's your...everything."

And her car. I could try to set out on foot. Maybe catch a friendly truck driver, though I imagine the incubus would have much better luck. The demon could take her back home leaving me to drive the rest of the way.

Alone.

Having to face my mother and tell her that...

"Stay," I sputtered, slamming my eyes closed and digging into the door handle with all my strength. This was the first time I had had to return home without either Eli or Mark at my side. *Completely, utterly alone.*

A hand brushed over my knee, causing me to shiver and gasp. But a hint of a smile was breaking apart the anger on Layla's lips. Blinking away the haze of grief in my eyes, I said softly, "The demon can stay."

"Ha." Ink punched into my shoulder without any force. "I knew you liked me. Your concerns are overwrought, my bond."

A snarl tried to catch in my throat, but I twisted it into a cough. Layla rose in her seat, turning her head to me and Ink. But before she collapsed into apologizing for the demon, she said, "Fine. You can come along. But will you sit your ass down and buckle up! Last thing any of us need is a bored county sheriff pulling us over because of you."

Ink snickered, as he always did, but gave in to her request. Without pause, he slipped into the seat behind Layla.

"And the seatbelt…" she said.

That caused a tut of his tongue, Ink tugging down the strap. When it locked into place, he said, "Interesting. You've been most intrigued by my tying you up. But your wishing me bound sounds most delightful."

Growling, Layla slapped at the radio, a Top Forty station filling the silence and wiping away the conversation. One hour down. Twenty-one more to go with an incubus in the backseat.

Chapter Six

The peace, what little there was, didn't last. Ink kept shifting his position in the backseat. At one point, his bare foot kicked into the back of my headrest. I spun around to find his other leg with a shoe on resting on the window ledge behind him. All I got for my annoyance and confusion at his contortions was a smirk.

"Traveling is so dreadfully boring!" the incubus whined like the proverbial five-year-old. I waited for him to ask if we were there already and to have Layla shout at him to sit down and shut up. His head popped in between the seats, Ink's chin pivoting as he said, "Why don't we make things interesting?"

Layla snorted and flared the fingers locked around the steering wheel. With a shrug, Ink slipped back into his seat, the belt retracting with a hard slap. He didn't stop gazing up at her, but not like a subject worshipping his queen. Ink looked more like a cat weighing whether he could get away with swatting a potted plant off the counter. It was hard to not shake the feeling that he was playing with her, and I had no idea if Layla realized it or not.

"What do demons find interesting?" I asked, jerking both the witch and the incubus to me.

"Oh, Cal..." Layla moaned. Had she already had this conversation with him? Or was I not even supposed to talk to the demonic half in this relationship?

"I wouldn't know," Ink said, "as I am not a demon."

"Fine, what do spirits of lust find interesting?" *Sex, you idiot. All he cares about, all he thinks about is sex.* Probably spends his days running through every permutation of putting tab A into slot B.

Is that the only thing that goes through his mind when he's around Layla? How her breasts tumble so far apart her nipples look cross-eyed when she's on her back? The way her ankle bone fits perfectly into a palm when holding her leg behind my head? Or how she gives this little squeeze when I first enter her, like a welcoming hug with her vagina?

Oh crap. Why is the demon smiling?

He cupped a hand under his chin, his fingers beating against his cheek like a metronome. In a curious voice, Ink said, "You."

"What about me?" I tried to wrench myself around and out of the conversation, but the demon's yellow-orange eyes burned in the mirror.

"You are interesting."

"Wha...? No, I'm not."

Even I knew it was a lie, my tongue flattening over my teeth as if to try and wash away the full truth. I'd spent so much time pretending I was normal. Not a werewolf. Not from a cult. Nope, just an average guy with a lot of collars and chains in the hall closet despite not having a dog.

I wanted it to be true, for me to be normal, average. *Boring.*

"Of course, you must be right. You are highly uninteresting," the incubus said, throwing his hands up and falling back into his seat.

What does he mean by that? I'm a goddamn werewolf. Every night my body sprouts fur and contorts. I grow a fucking tail, which is frankly weird as hell most days.

"Ignore him." Layla's cool voice tried to soothe me. She risked abandoning the steering wheel to cup my knee. "I intend to."

My head bobbed in agreement even as my skin prickled. It took less time than I feared getting my wolf to accept the stench of brimstone as friend. But the hackles rose from inside, wanting me to turn and test the demon's resolve against my teeth.

"Ah, so it's to be that winter solstice celebration all over again," Ink declared to himself in nearly a whisper, but it opened up the pits of hell in the car.

Layla and I both guiltily glanced to each other, then back at the third wheel behind us. "What are you talking about?" she said even though I knew she knew. We both knew.

The demon had been on her about some witch thing with the solstice. About how she had to cast a spell or study one. Layla had told him that on her way to greet the winter sun, she'd gotten caught in a snowstorm and missed it. Which was true, if I called my tongue *snow* and my penis *storm*. And all this time we'd thought the demon didn't have a clue.

"My bond," Ink said patronizingly. He reached over to stroke her forearm. "I am aware of every flush of your cheeks, every press of your lips, every grind, clench and lubrication of your—"

"Yes, okay, I get it!" she shouted, before blanching. "You know every...?"

"Time. Yes? Was it meant to be a secret? You both wear your desires on your faces as definitively as a carnival mask."

Wait, both...? "What are you talking about? You can't hear—"

Droll eyes met mine, Ink staring through me. "This morning you had a passing desire to lubricate your hand with butter to aid in pleasuring yourself."

Holy shit! I clenched my fists, my nails hardening to claws that wanted to impale his throat and stop him from talking. But the demon, aware I couldn't damage his skin enough to slit his vocal cords, wouldn't stop. "Though"—he frowned deep—"you abstained? I will never understand this incessant need to deny your desires. Would you like me to tell you of how he'd thought of pleasuring you in your car, my bond?"

"No, I would not," Layla shouted. "And stop reading Cal's or anyone else's desires."

Was I hyperventilating? I felt my tongue sliding out as if I'd been running all night in the wolf's fur. The damn demon knew every dirty thought in my head? He turned, casting a gleaming eye at me. Oh, that son of a...

"While I am incapable of providing transcendental pleasure to anyone but you, my bond, I'm afraid you cannot stop my innate ability to discern desires. And why would you wish it? I could tell you every eye that canvasses your body and has dark determinations with it."

"Will you fucking stop?! Stop…" Layla's shriek slammed into a wall. She knotted her jaw tight, her teeth locking together. But her nostrils flared and her lips opened into a rigid *O* as if she unleashed a scream without making a sound. She darted her rabid gaze around the car before landing it on her phone.

Without a care, she yanked it from the charger and tossed it back at Ink. "Here. Keep yourself busy with this."

"Ooh. My island requires many updates," the infernal incubus said to himself, already happily swiping through to his game. He turned back into that spoiled kid wasting time with Layla's phone.

Except he's not some naive child acting out for fun. He's had thousands of years to perfect his predator instincts. And it only took a few sentences for him to wedge fully between us. What if he wanted to do real harm? How could I stop him?

"You know what I need?" Layla said loudly to the quiet car. "Pancakes." She pivoted the car to the exit ramp, aiming us for a smaller town off the interstate.

All the while, I kept a lock on the demon quietly tending to digital sheep in the backseat.

* * * *

It wasn't until Layla pulled up next to the cement block of the half-flickering neon sign that I realized where we were. The letters for Mic's beamed across the gray sky like a beacon of greasy hope. At least that was how it'd looked to a scabbed-up kid without shoes fifteen years back.

"I hope I don't get tetanus from the door," Layla whispered to herself. She huddled a step closer, trying to avoid the pit in the concrete with cracked blacktop. All the parking lines had long been rubbed away by the years, leaving the few cars scattered like leaves tossed from a tree. I reached over to wrap an arm around her shoulders, the pounding in my heart calming at her touch…when the back of my hand smacked into an armpit.

Blinding teeth smiled at me, the demon quick to envelop his arm over both me and Layla. A flash shuddered in the back of my brain. I dropped my hold and slunk back, leaving Layla to walk in with the incubus on her.

Numb, I stared up at the fading roof. Its tiles were a grungy moss, though I didn't remember them being all that green in the past, either. Grit clung to the windows, only a circle smeared off every pane in the middle to let customers look in or gaze out at the unending world. The door swung open, a little bell tolling in response, and a pair of the kind of men who'd unironically own truck nuts walked out.

The world's least subtle leer trailed down Layla's body. *Yeah, she's hot. Okay, gorgeous, and not even her beloved purple hoodie can hide those curves. But why don't you…?*

Oh no.

The demon, the incubus who bragged about knowing everyone's desires, opened his mouth at the man drooling at Layla. My instincts drove me forward, wrenching my hands around the back of Ink's neck. I dug in with full claws to try to get him to shut his mouth. "Hey, why don't we get a table?" I practically shouted in his ear.

For a moment, the demon turned to me. I hadn't thought how sharp he looked before. In the world of wolves and witches, a man with a beak-like nose and deadly cheekbones didn't seem out of the ordinary. But standing beside men in Carhartt jackets and broken-in Wranglers, it was obvious how much Ink didn't belong. *Grab a pitchfork and build a pyre* didn't belong.

All that repressed anxiety shot through me like a bullet...which was something that small-town folks did to wolves getting too close to their livestock. Or worse. My hands wrung tighter to Ink's collar, practically shaking him in my grip.

"If you intend to manhandle me," he said loudly, "give me enough time to remove my trousers."

"Ha. Aren't you funny? Ha ha ha," I shrieked, hoping to pass off Ink's deadpan comment as a joke. The strangers hustled back to their truck like Cerberus was on their heels.

"If your intention was to cast suspicion upon yourself, you've quite succeeded," the demon kept on.

"What are you doing? You can't just... These people are dangerous."

With a pronounced shrug, Ink tossed my grip off him. I didn't let go. I couldn't. Even with all the supernatural muscle at my disposal, the demon brushed me off like a gnat. "As you can see, I am shaking in my cloven hooves over a peasant that had rather detailed thoughts on how he wished to slip my sausage betwixt his buns."

What? But they... That one had...

"Cal? I got us a table," Layla called, poking her head back out to the two of us standing in the open doorway. *When did she head in? Why didn't I realize she wasn't there with Ink? What the hell was wrong with me?*

"Are you okay?" she asked, her concern shoring up my spine.

"Yeah." I pushed past the demon and a thousand memories punched me in the gut at once. The smell of a million bacon sandwiches and fried eggs coalesced in the air, dragging me back to the first time I'd ever walked on carpet. It'd faded to the point the geometric pattern with the ancient neon colors was more of a drab olive and puce now.

The tables hadn't changed. They clustered beside a half wall topped by a small glass window with a silhouetted outline of covered wagons crossing the plains. But it was the booths, their crimson vinyl punctured so stuffing spilled out, that drew my attention and held it.

"Hey." A warm hand brushed up my waist under my jacket. A rush of air filled my lungs as if I emerged from a frozen lake. Gasping, I turned to Layla pointing in the direction of a table on the other side of the greasy spoon. The demon already sat there, face buried in the laminated menu.

I forced on a smile and jerked my head in the direction like I was the one guiding her. While Layla settled into the creaking chairs, I perched right on the edge. My thumb kept tugging on the edge of the menu, pulling apart the already fraying plastic as I failed to read anything on it.

"I know I said I wanted pancakes, but the sandwiches look good. What do you think?"

Why here? There were hundreds of small restaurants, cafés, or fast-food joints between the state borders. But out of every one of them, this was the one she'd stopped at. Because the demon wouldn't stop attacking until it forced us over? Or because the witch knew that this place was a piece of my past?

"Cal? What's going on—?"

"Hello." A woman approached the table and dropped water glasses in front of us. With the serving tray tipped to the side, she tugged out a pad and asked, "Is this your first time at Mic's?"

A poisonous guilt burst through me, but Layla didn't notice. She laid out her menu and pointed to the section of hot lunch options. "Yes. I was wondering, if I got the BLT, could I substitute the fries with a small stack of pancakes?"

The waitress smiled as if that was far from the craziest substitution request she'd gotten that day. "Sure, no problem," she said, writing it down while taking Layla's menu.

"Guess I wanted pancakes after all," Layla said to me.

"And you?" The waitress turned to me and my mouth dried.

"Meat," I whispered, my brain churning through a past loop I couldn't escape.

The waitress clicked her pen thrice and leaned closer. "What was that?"

We'd craved it in a way no human child could. Two days without and we'd been prepared to rip a squirrel to pieces with our bare hands. It didn't help that we couldn't read and had never been in a restaurant before. In the cult, no one had ever asked what I wanted — they just gave us food and if we didn't eat it, we starved.

"The meatloaf," I stuttered, remembering the slab of molded hamburger we'd dug into with our small fists. "I'd...like the meatloaf please."

"Sandwich or platter?"

"What's the difference?" I asked, but before she could explain, I said, "The sandwich, please."

"Okay." The woman made it obvious she wasn't a fan of me—not that I could blame her. But after writing down my order, she turned to Ink and her face lit up. "What would you like, Sir?" That wasn't a pleasant customer service *sir*, but a capitalized 'I want you to step on my face and chain me to the floor' Sir.

If Ink heard it… *Who am I kidding? He didn't just hear it—he probably knows every position the waitress wants him in.* But he didn't even blink at her. "I would like this apple pie placed upon a bowl of iced cream."

"Just a slice of pie with ice cream on top?" she asked.

"No. I wish to have an entire pie resting atop a bowl of ice cream. This rocky road sounds contentious but intriguing," the demon declared with a proud smile on.

"You want…?" The waitress' fantasies dried up fast in the face of his order. But as her gaze darted between all three of us, she wrote down Ink's pie request, gathered up the menus and beat a hasty retreat.

"Ink, we're in public," Layla groaned the second the woman was out of range.

The incubus gazed down. "I am clothed in trousers and an acceptable tunic. Even my toes are shod, see." He lifted his foot, shaking the shoe in Layla's face. Rather than fight him on it, she limply pushed his foot to the side until it landed with a heavy thud. It left the demon twisted in his chair and staring directly into Layla's face.

She didn't turn to him, but kept her focus on me, because Ink wasn't the only one acting weird. Layla's lips tugged back, her teeth parted so the tip of her tongue clicked against the bottom of her mouth to form my name. Cal.

Are you all right?

What's wrong?
Can I help?
Why aren't you normal?
Where's your brothers?
Can you keep quiet?

Chapter Seven

Fifteen years back...

We'd inhaled the little cracker stacks left in a small bowl on the table. When those ran out, Mark and I discovered that the strange little paper packets in the bowl were full of sugar. With our stomachs raging after a day and half walking out of the woods, we even ate the artificial sweeteners without more than a wrinkled nose. It wasn't enough.

Mom sat on the outside of the booth while the three of us scrabbled over the table and under it as if we had to catch our food. It was the first time I'd ever been on vinyl, or sat on a bench beside anyone. Eli's head popped up from below the table, his hair awkward and curled around his ears. I reached down to help him when the woman who'd been watching us approached.

She'd given us water, which was strange. And in a glass, which was stranger. We'd all avoided the large cups even though we were thirsty. If it wasn't boiled first, that got a beating. But Mark wrapped a hand around one of the rolled-up papers left on the table and dunked it into the cup. Entranced, we watched the ice swirl, pieces of the paper tumbling away.

"Tha's a fork!" Eli called, pointing at the surprise.

The paper gave way to reveal glinting metal hidden inside. Mark scooped the clumpy remains out of the cup and smeared it on the wall. "Who cares. There's a knife," he declared, hoisting the small blade up, leaving the fork and spoon behind.

A loud sigh burst from the woman in blue and all three of us froze. One thing we were all good at was knowing when adults got mad, and doing everything — including not breathing — until they moved on to hit someone else. Maybe she sensed we were scared, or maybe she thought she made her point, but the stranger put on a smile.

It didn't help.

Absently, I reached over to hold Eli's hand, cinching it tight in mine should we need to run. Mark dug his fingers so tight to the knife that his knuckles turned white. He hid it in his lap, staring out with the sides of his eyes. Only Mom was calm and smiling.

"Do you know what you want?" the stranger asked.

As one we turned to my mom. No, she's *our* mom now. That was what we were told to say if anyone asked. She held a big flat book in her hands and spread it across the table. We all peered at it from the side. I recognized a handful of letters, same as what was around the compound on crates and the like.

"What does that mean?" Mark asked. He pointed at the book, wondering about the letters same as me.

But Mom caught a look of shock on the stranger's face and leaned over to whisper, "She wants to know what you'd like to eat."

"Meat," Eli chirped quietly.

"Yeah, meat," I added, my stomach rumbling at the dream of filling it.

Soon all three of us were slapping our hands to the table shouting "Meat," at the top of our lungs. To get meat at the compound we had to catch it ourselves. Mark had got a rabbit once, but before he could even snap its neck, Eli adopted the bunny...for a couple days, then the Leader found and killed it for himself. We only ever got slivers of meat our moms fished from their weak stews. Some of us, anyway

"They..." My mom lashed out to pin all our hands to the table. In a flurry, she spun around and stood up as if to hide us. "They mean meatloaf," she said. "My kids really love meatloaf."

Eli leaned against me and whispered against my ear, "Wha's meatloaf?"

I shrugged, but the wary stranger made marks all over a white book and dashed away. It wasn't until the woman vanished behind a swinging door that Mom collapsed back to her chair. Dark eyes glared at the three of us. "You need to stay quiet."

I slapped one hand over my mouth and another over Eli's. Only his watery eyes and the tip of his nose were visible above my palm. We both nodded to my mom, then turned to Mark. He held his palm an inch before his mouth, his eyes glaring death, while he fiddled with the knife.

My mom reached over to hold Mark's hand and tugged it away from his mouth. Then she caught mine too and she shook both. "Not like... Not like that, okay.

You can talk, you can laugh. God, I hope you can laugh. But keep it to yourselves, okay? Secret brother time."

The side of my face burned hot from the snarl off Mark. I wasn't supposed to tell anyone about secret brother time. But my mom didn't count, right? Oh, I was gonna get a twisted ear or punch to the back of the head for that one later.

Whatever idle punishment Mark was dreaming up, he shifted tracks and turned to my Mom. "Will we really get meat?"

"Yes. That's how restaurants work. They have a list of foods you can eat and you pick one."

Any food we want, whenever? Like plums from the stand of trees by the creek?

"Do they have ice cream?" Eli gasped and I joined him. We'd only ever seen pictures of it against buildings and above the highways, people eating this strange creamy food that brought them pure joy.

"Ice cream ain't real," Mark said. To him it was the same as saying happiness wasn't real and we had no way to prove otherwise.

My mom inched closer to the table and lay down the broken finger she'd tied to a stick. Mark kept bouncing the post keeping his leg together against the wall, like he liked the pain. Reaching for his hand, Mom said, "If you're good, I'll see about getting you all a cone of chocolate and vanilla swirl."

That caused Mark to turn in shock, which was when Mom plucked the knife from his fingers. He scowled at the loss, but it didn't matter. Even I knew he had a knife that he'd made himself hidden in his pockets.

"Ice cream," Eli shouted in my ear while tugging on my sleeve. "Didja hear that? Real ice cream."

"I got that," I began, trying to be calm like Mom said. Though it was hard against Eli's blinding smile. I felt a laugh start which I was quick to swallow, my eyes automatically flitting to the side, when it dawned on me. I wouldn't get hit for laughing. Not by him, not by the tattlers. Not by no one.

It was like staring at a wall, seeing only the flat paint, then blinking and *boom*, a rainbow appears. The rainbow didn't come from anywhere—it was always there. I just hadn't seen it before.

Opening my mouth, I let the laugh slip free. Eli's eyes crinkled, his mouth open, but no sound escaped. Mark joined in with a harsher guffaw.

Diesel. Gun oil. Salted pork. Leather.

The scents punched through the air, striking me and the other werewolves at once. We didn't look around—we knew better than to risk catching his eye. As one we hunkered together, sliding tighter to the window. I grabbed Eli's hand, his fingers cold and limp, then reached for Mark. He caught me first, the whole of his arm shaking. Or maybe mine was.

We'd walked for so long that we couldn't stand. Slept in the dirt by the road to hide our scents. Gone hungry to the point my eyeballs ached. But it wasn't enough. He'd found us.

A shadow loomed over us all. I tried to reach for my mom but she'd gone rigid, her eyes fixed on the far wall. None of us breathed. I doubted our hearts even beat. All we could do was wait for the first slap, the second, then the belt.

"Hey, Doris!" a strange voice shouted from the darkness.

I risked taking another sniff. *Diesel. Gun oil. Salted pork. Leather. And candy?* That wasn't him. Fighting every instinct in my body, I darted my gaze out into the restaurant. A man with cherry red cheeks and a beard of snow stood in the middle. He threw his arms open wide and wrapped them around a woman in blue.

It wasn't him. Oh, my moon, it wasn't him.

A strange laugh that felt more like a scream burst from me. It woke my mom up, who turned around and spotted the older, rounder man heaving his belly around in a laugh. "Blessed be," she gasped and clasped her hands together in a prayer. Tears stained her cheeks, and I knew why. If he caught us, if he found us, we'd be dragged back, but my mom…he'd kill her in front of us. She'd never told me what would happen if we were found. She didn't have to.

"It's okay," Mom said, patting Mark's head and massaging my shoulder. "We're in farm country. People will smell like… It's okay."

Mark broke first, snatching up the dropped knife, then jamming it into the brickwork below the windowsill. He didn't say anything, just kept slamming at the blade's handle so it bounced in place. I tried to shake off the tremble in my hands and find that laugh I'd lost. Absently, I brushed at my nose, trying to push away the stench of home. *What used to be home.*

A new smell reached me, of ammonia and fear. Without looking down, I turned to Eli who was still pale white and pressing his lips so tightly together they looked about to burst. *Crap.* "Mom." Skidding along the booth while keeping Eli's hand in mine, I tugged on the sleeve of her shirt. "Can you move?"

She reached out, keeping me penned in place. "Where do you think you're going?"

"Eli's…" I risked glancing back and took a deep breath. My mom followed suit, no doubt smelling the same.

"I can…" she started while standing up to let us slide out of the urine-soaked booth. "No, you're both too old. Cal, can you take him to the bathroom?"

I nodded, even while uncertain where I could find a stream or river. But my mom pointed me in the direction of a door with a blue man on it. "It'll be okay, Eli," she said rubbing his thin back.

Raising my head to try to ignore the smell and the squishy sound of Eli's legs rubbing together, I guided him for the strange door and walked into another new world. An entire row of sinks ran the entire wall. At the compound, we only had one in the kitchen and only a handful could use it.

The gleam off the mirrors caught me, but I turned my back to focus on Eli in wet pants. "Can you…do you need me to help you out of them?" I asked while pointing to his jeans. Numb, Eli unhooked the button and let them fall to the floor. I picked up the damp pair and carried them to the sink.

Warm water poured from the tap, another miracle that nearly sent me yelping when it turned too hot. Only the sound of rushing, magical water echoed off the stone walls. Eli stood in the middle of the room, half naked, with his hands clenched to his bare thighs.

I tried to find a soap bar left by the fancy sinks, but there was nothing, not even slivers. Only some strange pink liquid trapped inside a box hung by them, but I wasn't going near it. The hunters would dye their poisons pink so the wolves wouldn't eat it by mistake.

Eli's pants, wetter than before, hung in my hands. I didn't know what to do. There was a trash can by the door. Maybe I could pick a few napkins out to help dry them. Leaning over the silver bin, I tried to balance on a box just above the trash. My elbow slipped and rammed into a button.

Hot air burst across my head, snapping me out of the trash. It roared like a plane passing overhead. Eli covered his ears, his eyes wide, but I knew how to dry his pants. Placing them over the mouth of the pipe, I pushed the button and held on. Air filled the twin legs of his jeans, tossing them about like flags on the wind.

When the air came to a stop, I checked the crotch of his jeans and gave another push. This didn't seem to be the miracle answer I'd hoped for. Eli's pants remained stubbornly damp so I slammed the button again, then a fourth time hoping the air would come out hotter and faster. *Get rid of his accident. Wipe away the shame from it. Clean him up so I don't have to think about how bad I feel.*

Felt.

We're out and we're never going back.

"Cal…?" Eli's soft voice called from behind.

Oh shit. Fur and claws reflected in the button's warped surface. I clenched my toes and willed away the beast inside when Eli padded over and took his pants away. He began to slip them on while I folded my fists and glared at the ground.

"How's it…okay?"

"I've sat in worse," he said, and a garbled laugh broke from me. We all had. Piss was better than shit, which was better than blood.

The bathroom door burst open. I reared back, raising my hands as if they could do any damage, but it was Mark who strolled in. He slammed both hands to his hips and asked, "What the shit is taking you two so long? Mom's having a fit."

An angry Mark was oddly assuring, like tracks after a snowstorm. We knew exactly what to expect when he was in that mood.

"We're done, okay. Keep your fur on," I said, glaring back at him. My older brother sneered back, and we both reached for the door at the same time.

It was Eli who didn't move, who kept looking at the mirror as if he feared to find a monster lurking inside. "Will he find us?" he asked in *that* voice. The voice we used when huddled together at night trying to find any way to survive without having to kill each other. The voice that cut right through me.

"No," I said, shaking my head and turning to calm Eli.

"I hope he does," Mark snarled, and he extended his hands, the claws coming on instinct.

"No, you don't," I chided him before turning to the youngest. "It's okay, Eli. We've lost him. Mom said as much, remember. Back at that truck place with all the maps." I reached for my brother, trying to clasp him in an assuring hug. Eli was as stiff as a board, refusing to raise his hands, so I held him tighter.

"One day..." Mark paced about the room. He fished the homemade knife from his pocket and started to flick it around. "I'm gonna kill him."

I snorted at the thought. The asshole was a full-grown wolf with teeth bigger than our fingers. Even together we couldn't hope to hurt him. "Sure you will," I said, rolling my eyes.

"I'll gut him with this knife. Tear out his throat, and let it bake on the stones like jerky." Madness flooded through Mark, but worse than that, he was deadly serious. Swiping the blade through the air, he sneered, as if he was slicing our father to bits.

I caught his elbow and tossed his hand back. It kept the knife from hurting anyone, especially Eli. "Will you shut the hell up? We got to keep running, not fighting. And if you start making all these threats, you're gonna make my… You'll piss Mom off."

Sense slipped through Mark's bravado. He always had it by the truckloads, which the asshole would then try to beat out of him. But even he knew if we tried to claw, our nails would break. If we tried to bite, our teeth would shatter. Our only hope was running and never looking back. With a scowl, Mark pocketed his knife and left the bathroom.

I reached to take Eli's hand and help him back to the table. Hopefully there'd be food waiting for us, maybe even that ice cream we'd dreamed about. It'd cheer anyone up through wet pants.

As we passed the mirrors, Eli turned to stare at his face. Instead of the sweet, cautious boy I'd known, the visage hardened to something sharper than even our father's cruel look. "I'll do it, Cal. I'll kill him. And it'll hurt. Bad."

Where was I?

The sound of water gushing from pipes snapped me out of the memory and I found myself standing in that same bathroom. I wrenched my neck around, expecting to find Eli's tiny jeans stuck to the hand dryer. But they weren't there because my younger brother was gone. Killed by the bastard he swore he'd kill.

I'm sorry I didn't get him first, Eli. I'm sorry I failed to protect you.

Layla. I'd left her at the table. She was probably worried, about to send the demon in to find me. Stiff-legged, I pushed open the door and didn't look at the small booth where a terrified family had gotten their start at a new life.

Chapter Eight

Layla cut off a pat of butter and hid it in her pancake stack. She plunged her fork into the top while chewing on a slip of bacon that had fallen from her sandwich. When she picked up the pitcher to drench the pancakes in syrup, she glanced up at me.

"Where's Ink?" I said first, stumbling to my chair and wrapping a hand around my sandwich. It wasn't until I had it in my fingers that I realized it was open-faced and I was supposed to eat it with a fork. Too late now.

Tipping her head to the side, Layla said, "He spotted the buffet and ran for it. Meanwhile…"

Sure enough, an entire apple pie lay in a bowl of ice cream. They'd had to pull out what looked like those giant ones that held massive salads just to fit it. It looked like there was easily a full quart of ice cream underneath the pie.

Layla dipped the edge of her fork into the abandoned dessert and brought a piece of the pie and ice cream combo to her lips. At my look, she said through the food, "It's not fair. He gets to eat all that and still look like…"

A burn rose in my gut and I lay my soggy bread and crumbling meatloaf back on the table.

"Though you get to, too, with all that muscles and stuff." Her voice wobbled in uncertainty, but I caught her gaze homing under my clothing. The demon wasn't the only one with a supernatural build.

It'd be nice to sit there lapping up her compliments, but her fork dropped and so too went the boom. "You okay? You just got up and wandered off, looked like you were in a trance."

"I'd…" Knitting my fingers together, I stared at the mud under my nails, remnants from my last shift I'd failed to scrub away. "I went to the bathroom," I said.

"Oh."

We'd spent so much time lying it came naturally. There was this other me, the one from a loving home who'd gone to kindergarten and learned to tie his shoes along with the alphabet. The one who couldn't go to slumber parties or have friends over cause his mom was super strict. The public one who didn't know what a cult was, or suffered regular night panics about a man reeking of diesel leaping through his window.

Sometimes people sensed the mask. They'd get cold, realize we weren't telling the whole truth, or maybe not even talk to us again. But no one ever pushed it, as if they knew it was too dangerous to ask for more.

"We came here," I whispered. "When we first escaped."

I could lie to so many people — friends, coworkers, professors, bosses, girlfriends — often without even a second thought. It was to protect them, I'd tell myself.

What if my father found and tortured them? But he was gone, and I still kept lying.

No more.

"Our first time in a restaurant. First time inside any place that wasn't at the compound."

Fingers brushed over mine. I couldn't feel them, but I watched her soft skin fold around the back of mine. Opening my hand, I caught her fingers between mine and held tight.

"We ate so much meatloaf that night I thought I was gonna hurl. My mom, she...didn't have any money. We didn't even understand what money was."

So when the check had come, she'd told us all to shift in the bathroom and run out through the back. We'd thought nothing of it. I hadn't figured out what we'd done until I'd been much older after we'd faced down landlords and debt collectors who'd come to the wolf's door.

"Hey," Layla called to me, brushing her hand under my chin. I looked up into her bright eyes brimming with concerned tears. "You did what you had to to survive. It's not your fault, or hers."

"I don't like to use that excuse," I said. "It becomes a blank check so easy." She didn't understand. How could she? How could anyone?

I bottled my old thoughts deep inside and reached across the table to cup her cheek. "I'm fine. Really. Just all this pack business dredging up old history."

She nodded her head in agreement, but narrowed her eyes. They knew I was doing it again, putting up the lie for the sake of others. Everyone always needed protecting. If I stopped, they died.

Slipping away from her, I reached for a fork to eat the meatloaf that was worse than I remembered. "Cal."

Layla's soft voice caressed my ear. The wolf loved hearing her say my name. The human was rather partial to it as well.

"Your mom's gonna be okay."

I wanted to believe her so fervently. For her words to be law and alter the course of fate itself. But my mistake, my failure, had pulled all of us back into the crosshairs of pack politics. And no one walked away from that unscathed.

"We should...eat. Then hit the road. Got a lot of miles still to go." I made a mental note to add the cost of a meatloaf dinner from fifteen years ago to the tip, when a massive plate landed beside the sinking pie.

A great smile strained the demon's lips, and he began to shovel beets and cottage cheese onto his apple ice cream disaster. "This is a fantastic comestible establishment. No wren's livers or ox tongues, but the vegetable array is astonishing despite the winter months upon us."

"I am never taking you out to eat ever again," Layla said, horrified as the incubus began to cram great spoonfuls of pie, beets and ice cream into his mouth. For his part, the demon shrugged, either unaware of the pain he caused, or fully conscious that she could never escape him.

How many more romantic dinners in my future would include a demon eating the dessert and appetizer courses in one trough? Stabbing into the meatloaf, my hunger gone, I tried to focus on the upcoming drive and what I'd find in Santa Fe. But my mind kept flitting back to Layla with the hot shower water beading across her skin.

Chapter Nine

When I hit the switch, the dome light above the door and a sconce by the bed both lit up. The motel room had that stench of cigarettes baked into old caulk and moldy carpet. With a lot of dark browns in the plywood furniture and sickening olive greens for the walls, it was doubtful the place had been redecorated in my lifetime.

"How's it look?" Layla asked from behind, pressing her hand to my back and grazing my shoulder with her cheek. She couldn't see anything past the old door that took five swipes of the key card to let us in.

"There aren't any roach armies," I said, taking a step deeper inside. The bed looked like it was printed on cardboard. I'd swear the edges were corrugated, but at least it supported my duffel bag. Stretching the crick in my neck that had started when we left Iowa, I turned to face Layla.

Even after the past ten hours in the car, she glowed. Motel light would be cruel to Aphrodite herself, but

Layla's smile overpowered the sallow cast above. I reached for her without thinking, snagging my hand on her purse. That spell book inside bounced against my knuckles, but I didn't care.

Pulling myself to her like a comet approaching the sun, I darted my fingers through her hair and leaned down to kiss her.

"Is this the brothel?"

A groan rolled from her lips while I faced the demon strolling in without a care in the world. He'd 'entertained' us for most of the trip. It was hard to say if it was on purpose or part of his perverse joy in making everyone around him uncomfortable. Whatever the reason, all I wanted was to close my eyes and not have to see his annoyingly handsome face for a few hours.

I expected Layla to whip around and chastise him, but she shook her head. Had he worn her down too? Rolling my arm around her shoulder, I pressed Layla close to my side as we walked into the room. There wasn't far to go or much to see in the *discount suite*. A chest of drawers that had probably once acted as a cradle for a litter of possums held up the square TV. Beside it was a table with a lamp nailed to the top. A folding chair sat next to the table, because even a cheap plywood one was too much to expect from Econo-Snooze.

Layla chucked her bag and purse onto the bed, both of us watching the mattress fold in on itself. For a moment, I feared it'd keep going until the entire bed sucked into a black hole. It'd match my life. Despite the hours with my long legs cramped in the car, I stumbled to the mattress and half-sat. The pressure built on my hip and I stared out through the partially drawn blinds. The sun had stained them to a vomit yellow and left a quarter of the bottoms cracked and broken like bones left in the desert.

Mark told me it was a coyote skeleton. But the legs were too thick, the skull's nose too long. There've been rumors of another wolf pack in the area. One that didn't like outsiders encroaching on their territory. I agreed with Mark, just a coyote, despite what my nose told me. Coyotes didn't smell like cologne and denim.

We didn't tell Eli. We didn't want him to worry.

And now the pack knew about Mom. About me, and probably Mark too. Would they try to force us into their ranks? I wouldn't do it. I'd rather die than submit to an alpha, any alpha.

What about Mom?

"Don't eat that!" Layla shouted, shaking me from my thoughts.

Ink unwrapped one of the small complimentary soaps left in the bathroom, placed the ivory edge to his teeth and bit down. "Hm," he said, "these confections are rather bitter." As he talked, bubbles rolled off his tongue to coat his muzzle.

This was the sexy incubus that posed a threat? He looked like a grade schooler struggling to not eat glue. I glanced to Layla, expecting her to run over and make him spit out the soap. But she slumped her shoulders and turned away. Unperturbed, Ink bit off another chunk and peered around the room.

"What's that for?" he asked, gesturing with the half-gone soap bar.

"The bucket?" I stared at the pseudo-wood paneling around the container. "To get ice from the machine…"

"There's a machine that creates ice?" Ink's eyes widened. He scooped the bucket up and kept lifting the lid.

Smiling, Layla turned to him. "It's somewhere in the motel. A huge machine full of ice. Why don't you go find it?"

His smile grew, the amber eyes sharpening and joy overrunning his features. The childlike fool from before completely vanished. A man whose every beat of his heart and breath from his lungs screamed sex stood before me instead. "This I must see," Ink declared as if an ice machine were the most amazing thing in the world.

I glanced at Layla, expecting her to melt from the incubus' confident stride. But she'd busied herself in her bag, tugging out her sleepwear. When the door closed, locking Ink out of the room, she tossed her head back and sighed. "Finally."

In one smooth move, Layla shoved her bag to the head of the bed and collapsed face-first into the mattress. I snickered to myself and sat discretely on the edge. "He is so fucking exhausting sometimes," she muttered against the dusky rose comforter.

"I don't know how, but if he tries to start another round of ninety-nine bottles tomorrow, I will cut him into tiny pieces," I declared.

Leaning to the side, Layla glanced up at me. "I'll help," she said, both of us laughing at the empty threat. She winced while turning and reached for her shoulder, but I beat her to it. Without pause, I dug into the knotted muscle, trying to unwind the tension that only driving for a day could cause.

At first, she bit into her bottom lip, her body swaying to encourage my massage to the right spot. But when I hit the motherlode, Layla gasped. "Fuck, yes! That, right there."

Heat burst over my cheeks and in my gut. Focusing on healing her instead of the flush working down my spine, I shifted my legs wider so one reached to the floor. Then Layla began to pant. And moan.

She'd closed her eyelids, the lashes fluttering with every press of my thumbs. Her lids shifted, the deeper hue drawing me in, demanding I kiss her so hard they fly open in surprise. I had to feel her body shiver in my arms, her breasts press to my chest, and her nails slice down my back.

Damn it. A pinch snagged where the fold of my jeans wouldn't give for my rising cock. I didn't want to abandon my massage, so I tried flailing my leg out, hoping that'd be enough room for my pinched erection to slide free. I don't know why. It never worked.

"Oh, here," Layla said. Her gaze burned into me as she rose from the bed and dug her fingers into my shoulders. "Your turn," she declared.

She was so much better at it than me. Hooking her thumbs into where the trapezius met my collar, she fluttered her fingers up the back of my neck. The delicate touch, so light at first that I barely felt it, began to build. I waited in anticipation for her to dance her fingers up my vertebrae and trail back down, taking my anxiety with them.

Serenity washed over my body, the calming waves taking away the burning node I'd crammed every awkward emotion into for the past day. I ached for surrender, to fall onto the bed and have her brush away the tension knots in my body. Giving in to the idea, I began to crawl on all fours onto the bed.

I'd hooked one knee onto the mattress, the other prepared to join it, when the wolf took over. It didn't want to rest. It wanted…

Layla gasping for oxygen below me. My hips slamming into her ass as she rocks on her knees. My hands digging into her shoulder to pull her deeper onto my cock. And my teeth scraping down her back, ready to plunge –

My phone burst to life, snapping away the wolf's slobbering hunger. I skittered with a full erection to check even as I realized what the sound was. A cute little *bing-bong* could only mean one thing – full moon soon.

When I heard it again, I stared at my phone. I'd already closed out of the app, so what was...?

With her cheeks pink, Layla dug her phone out of her purse. She prodded at the same app, canceling the same warning...a warning only werewolves needed.

"Why do you have a moon tracker?" I asked.

She shrugged one shoulder and fiddled with her phone. "I thought it'd be smart to warn me."

Pain struck me in the gut. It was fair. The wolf can be...intimidating, to put it mildly. I couldn't blame her, but I also couldn't escape the feeling of betrayal. I'd never told a girlfriend the whole werewolf issue before. I'd always feared her fearing me.

"Warn you about...?" The last word clogged in my throat. *Warn her about me.*

Layla dropped her phone into her bag, then the whole thing onto the floor. She brushed her palm to my cheek, combing her fingers through my hair. The warm breath from her lips set off both a prickle of shame in me and an ache in the wolf.

Her bottom lip crested against my skin, setting off a tremble as I struggled to keep myself at bay. In a soft voice, she said, "I like to know when I should wear my tearaway underwear."

Taking her chin in my hand, I pulled Layla to me. I pried her lips apart with my tongue, the ache bursting to an inescapable need to taste her. The scent of her drenched down my throat, transforming into the flavor of lightning striking the midnight dunes.

She tugged off my shirt, letting her nails scratch up my back. I couldn't escape her kiss. The heat of her lips, the hard pressure trying to take control. I needed more. I needed to...

My teeth grazed her jaw and Layla froze in reaching for my jeans. I didn't know what I was doing, only the bulging ache to do it. A whimper slipped from her. The exact same one I'd heard whenever she'd leap into a too-cold shower, when I'd press my frozen hands to her back, when I'd suck on her clit.

I bit down. The strength of her jaw and the supple fall of her cheek filled my mouth. Pain throbbed from my back molars, almost breaking me off, when Layla cried out, "Do it! Again!"

Her face flushed so hot the air radiated off her cheek. I brushed my nose along the hollow of it, tracing under the bone while watching white marks rise against her soft brown skin. My bite was deeper than I had meant.

Shame pounded back the wolf, sending me scampering to my feet. But Layla followed, her hands hooked to my belt loops. The whole trip I'd had to pretend I wasn't mesmerized by her breasts peeking out from under her top. Had to grit my jaw and act as if I didn't want to squeeze both in my hands.

Now, they bounced in her hop from the bed to my side, hypnotizing me. "Cal...?" she whispered, her breath twisting in my ear along with my name.

Oh fuck! Popping open my jeans, Layla strained her hand down the front and gripped me with all her reach.

A snarl roared from inside. The wolf was mad that I had stopped. The wolf needed her. I pushed Layla's back to the wall, ignoring the bed a foot away. Her eyes widened when she struck it, but she cinched her hand tighter to my cock and began to pump.

I took her shoulder in my jaws and bit. Layla locked her grip around my cock, squeezing and setting off another growl. But it was the moan of pleasure from her perfect lips that controlled me. She tried to pump my cock while I nipped my teeth across her chest. An urge to rip her shirt off with my fangs pounded in my head.

Holy hell!

She flicked her thumb over the head of my cock, sending my grip on reality reeling. I grabbed her wrist and pinned her to the wall. Before I could hunt out the other, she tugged off my jeans, letting the baggy pair fall to the ground.

I stood in nothing but my bare ass and socks while she was fully clothed. The beast and his beauty. Any other time of the month, I'd carry her to the bed. Kiss down her arms, up her legs, fill my mouth with her breasts.

But the wolf wasn't gentle. And it certainly wasn't slow.

Holding both her hands to the wall, I nudged Layla's legs apart with my knee. As she slid lower, a surprise giggle escaping, I clamped one palm to both her wrists and tugged on her trousers. *Thank you, whoever invented yoga pants.* No fucking buttons, no zippers, no ties, and I got to enjoy her perfect bubble ass twenty-four seven.

I tugged them to her knees, not caring to get her naked, only needing to have her. Curling my fingers over the strip of her panties, a shudder of delight shook through me as I felt the full slick of her arousal across my knuckles. "Tell me these are the tearaways," I grunted, puffing my words against her neck.

Layla, splayed against the wall, turned to me. Her eyes sparked mischief as she said, "Depends on how hard you pull."

Fuck! I doubled my grip, prepared to test the seams of the cotton keeping me from her, when a thud landed outside the door. Was it the demon? Had he finished with his ice retrieval?

Whipping my head up, I tried to train my human ears to track the sound. If it was Ink, he was being louder than usual.

"What is it?" Layla asked. She'd turned her head, revealing the white marks of my bite.

I had done that to her without thought, without asking. What if she desired something else? What if she desired someone else?

"Cal?" she prompted, her eyebrows folding in confusion. Her hands slipped from my grip and I stumbled away from her waiting and willing body. Pain spidered up my jaw, splintering into a headache. The wolf was pissed beyond measure. It wanted its mate. But watching Layla drop her hands to her sides as if she were about to pull up her pants sent me reeling.

I tugged off my socks, leaving me fully naked, while I said, "The moon. The wolf. I have to…I need to-to change."

"Now?" she shouted, causing me to wince.

No, not now! Look at her! Lips red as a cherry, cheeks glistening in anticipation, clothing askew and breasts heaving from hunger. She wants you.

But did she desire me?

76

"So-sorry," I shouted, yanking open the door without even checking to see if anyone was walking through the hall. If there was, they'd get to watch a naked man's body twisting into a giant gray wolf, running away like a coward.

Chapter Ten

Frozen dirt packed into the ground by the churning of tractor wheels. The tips of dead grass frosted by a late snow. The stench of diesel fuel and the herd of pigs in the truck on the breeze. Pinpricks of light dimmed in the distance the farther I slipped over the flat horizon.

Under the black skies with stars straining against the town's glare a mile back, it was as if all of existence faded away. The din of traffic speeding on the highway with only their bug-smeared headlights vanished to a light wind. All my ears could pick up was my heart and paws beating the same steady drum cadence.

Wind of my making rippled through my fur, but I shook off the cold. At the end of my snout, I could barely see the puffs of steam rising from my nostrils. With the moon behind, and nothing but eternal indigo ahead, I stared at my breath.

What are we doing?

My wolf was pleased to run, to stretch the muscles that'd been cramped not in a car but by my human skin.

But it wanted me to turn around and run back to the motel. To her.

We can go back.

And if he's already replaced me?

The wolf had no answer to that. It didn't go in much for higher thought, preferring instinct and reaction. The reflexes and heightened senses were nice, but when it came to decision-making it knew who to bow to.

We can take our turn.

That'd been the plan. For a month, she'd choose between the two of us. I barely even saw the demon aside from when stopping by her place. But if she was already growing tired of me, of all of this...

I flexed my paw into the ground, slicing the claws deep into the dirt. The last time she'd faced paws like that, she'd nearly died.

I hadn't changed in front of her since. Who wouldn't look upon bones rippling, skin snapping, and see a monster? It came from a monster.

We should turn back. The moon is falling.

There the wolf took precedence. I could maintain this form even in daylight, but people driving into work would question a wolf running through their streets. And others in the motel stumbling for their free breakfast would probably dash for a shotgun.

I needed to return before anyone saw me.

In a heartbeat, the wolf pivoted. My right paw had planted deep into the cold soil when the hair down my back stood up. Something was wrong.

My ears shifted, homing in on a sound far in the distance. I raised my head and turned to look back to the south. A massive light of blue and red burst over the horizon.

What was that?

Both wolf and man ran for it. As I climbed up the rare hill in Kansas, the mass of incoherent noise broke into sounds. A woman screamed, not in pain but anger. She said something, but I couldn't make it out.

Oh shit! A gunshot ripped through the air, setting off a yelp in my throat. My tail dropped between my legs, phantom pains shooting through my old bullet wound. The wolf wanted me to turn around, but I gritted my teeth, spittle dripping from my lips and freezing on my coat.

"You sonnofabitch!" the woman shouted. She wasn't dead. Or she was the one shooting. Hard to say.

I launched myself up the hill. A single car cast its harsh headlights over a bloody scene. The silhouette of a woman clutched her leg as she limped back from two men armed with shotguns.

"Stand down," one ordered, raising the barrel higher.

The woman paused in escaping, but she stood taller. Wings of gold erupted from her back. Even in the dark shadows of the night, they glowed, every speck of firelight sparkling as she flapped.

"Fuck you," she shouted and raised her hand.

A rumble shook below my feet. Deep within the earth, I felt the ground, the very grains of dirt shattering apart. The woman flitted her golden wings wide and snapped her open palm at the men.

They stumbled back, their guns aiming wildly into the air. A pitiful *poof* of sand, like a kid blowing off dust, burst from the ground.

"Ugh! I hate this fucking terrain!" she screamed.

Another shot rang out, this one tearing through her wing. The left crumpled, golden sparks careening past to highlight the bullet's path. A heart-wrenching shriek of pain burst from the woman and she fell to her knees.

I watched, too far away to do anything, as the second man aimed his gun at the helpless woman.

No!

A net spidered through the air, striking the woman. The weights attached to it swung back, slamming into her body and knotting together until she fell to the dirt. She screamed at them, trying to raise the ground to do her bidding, but the men laughed at their captured prey.

It was their turn.

Both men tucked their guns to their shoulders, one holding back while the other reached for the net to drag the woman away. I leaped for the arm. In that second, I smelled not only their soap and cologne, but the coffee they'd stopped for, the powdered sugar that had fallen in his lap and the utter cruelty in his heart.

All four hundred pounds of me landed on the man's spine. He screamed in shock and pain as I knocked him to the ground. Aware of the threat in his hand, I locked my jaws around his shoulder and bit. Not deep enough to sever any muscle or arteries, but the pain sundered straight to his palm, casting off the gun.

The other man heard his companion. He stopped reaching for the net and turned. They made it look easy in action movies, to slip the gun off its harness, place it to the eye, aim and fire. Real life never worked that well. In reaching for his shotgun, the man in the suit smacked his elbow into the butt.

It sent him twisting around to catch it, taking his eyes off me. Digging my front paws into the ground, I shifted my stance and launched onto him. He tried to dart away, but his foot caught in the dirt. I collapsed the man like a sack of flour, his head striking the frozen ground harder than a cement brick.

Dimness rolled across his eyes, the pain shattering whatever resolve he had to finish me. I had no intention of killing him, but I needed him gone. Both of them.

Opening my jaws, I let the pent-up saliva from my run drip onto his face. It crystalized in the sharp winter air, shocking him back into realizing a wolf with a head the size of a lion's was about to rip his throat open.

"*Shiiiit!*" he screamed, bringing his arm up to protect his face.

I wished I could talk, to tell him to get out of here or I'd eat them both. But there was no magic telekinesis I could use to communicate while in wolf form. Even other werewolf's howls sounded like a vague complaining whine or whoop of joy to my ears.

Raising my paw so the man would see it, I crushed the full weight of it onto his shoulder. His eyes opened wide and I moved to take a step off, to let both of them flee into the night, when the first man raised his gun and cocked it.

Fuck.

"Don't you goddamn even!"

I spun from the armed man to find the woman standing with the other gun in her hands. The net clung to her body, pinning her wings in place, but her entire face was twisted in a snarl that said she wasn't backing down for anything. *Wait.* That nose looked familiar.

"Put it down," she said. "Put it down or my friend eats yours, then I fill you with a...how many's this carry? A dozen or so holes sound good?"

I rippled my lips in a snarl, trying to emphasize her threat. Reaching for the man's head, I bounced the tip of my fangs into his wide forehead, feeling his panicking squeals reverberate through my jaw.

With a sneer, the other man hurled his gun away. It caught on the hill and rolled farther than either of us could reach. "Now, how about you…?" the woman began, when her leg buckled. She began to fall and on instinct I ran to her.

It wasn't until I nearly had her elbow on my back that I realized my mistake — the men ran for their car. They wasted no time throwing it into reverse, the man I could have eaten having to run to leap into the passenger side rolling without him. An urge to bark at it rose in my genes, but I held rigid.

For whatever reason, the men didn't drive forward to crush us. Instead, they peeled out, dust rising over the horizon to mark their return to the highway. I could track them, if I had a car and there wasn't a woman bleeding on my coat.

Laying my ears back to tell her I was a friendly giant wolf, I turned to the woman…and all the pieces clicked into place.

Skin the color of a virgin desert lit by the rising sun, features thin and sharp, a smile that never stopped twisting like the sidewinder and eyes little more than pinpricks until they opened to a striking black under the moon. I watched her struggle to the ground, my wolf melting away to my human form.

Her name kept repeating in my head, but it wasn't until I ran my tongue over flat teeth that I said, "Mikki?"

"Hey, Cal. Long time," she said, brushing back her long purple and red hair. "I see you're still a werewolf."

"It's not an easy thing to stop being," I said. The heat of battle rushed through my veins, but it wouldn't last long against the January cold of midnight.

"Fuck knows you tried..." she continued before her face knotted up in agony. "Gaia take those motherfuckers and shove red hot stalactites up their anuses!"

"What were they doing? Why were they chasing you? What happened?" I reached for her leg, inspecting it for damage. The tattered remains of her dress clung to the wound. Dark blood dripped across the ripped skin, making it impossible to get a sense of how bad it was.

"Is this really the time?" Mikki asked. "I'm usually all for a catch-up, but I don't know if I'll be much for conversation if I don't — *sonofa* — !"

"Here." I planted my hands on the ground, the frozen ground shocking my naked palms. "Climb on my back," I said, already starting the shift. One was exhausting enough, but two in one night would drain my body to famine levels. *Guess I'll be eating through my entire cache of candy tonight.*

Mikki looked up from her gushing wound, her face twisted in pain. "Are you sure that's...? Ah! Okay, all aboard the Calvin Express. Toot toot!" she said, rolling her body over mine.

I raised up slowly, hoping Mikki would know to grip on. She ruffled her fingers through my fur, locking over my shoulders. Giving a short test walk, I made certain she was secure, then launched into a full-on run. All the while, her hot blood oozed through my fur and my breath crystalized in the air.

Hang on, Mikki. I know someone who can help... assuming she's not impaled on a demon right now.

Chapter Eleven

Lashing forward, I bashed my foot into the motel door. It rattled on the hinges, hopefully telling Layla I needed her to answer it. Preferably before anyone wandered down the hall and noticed a naked man carrying a bleeding woman. Mikki was conscious and kicking up her usual level of swearing at the world, but I kept having to shake her to get her to focus. And my hand wouldn't stop slipping from her leg. Every time I adjusted, I left more crimson-stained handprints on her dress.

"Layla..." I risked my voice. "Can you open the door?"

"Coming," she called with a laugh. I felt certain she'd have that 'just rolled off him' flush to her cheeks. "We were going to—"

Her words stopped dead, drawing me to find her in a cottony tank top and boy shorts—her pajamas. *Whew.* "This is Mikki," I said, dashing inside past Layla. She stood beside the door, clinging to it in confusion.

Perched on the edge of the chair was the demon exuding the aura of a man who'd just taken a drag of a cigarette.

Ink tipped two fingers at me in a strange wave-threat. "I see you had a productive run."

Mikki moaned in my arms, pulling me from him. "She's hurt, bad," I said, twisting around to show the length of her blood trailing from her leg down mine.

"Holy fuck!" Layla shouted. The door slammed so hard it nearly bounced free. Without pause, Layla ran to my side. "What happened? Have you stopped the bleeding? I might have some silver nitrate in my purse's first aid kit."

Ink gave a solitary cough and pointed to the bag.

Slapping her forehead, Layla winced. She directed me to place Mikki on the bed and dug out her spell book. That caught Mikki's waning attention.

"She's a witch?"

The flying pages paused and Layla spat out the Sharpie's cap. "Yeah. So what? Cal, can you clean up the wound for my ward?"

The blood flow had slowed enough that I probably could. *Have to wash and dry it as fast as possible before it starts again.* I dashed into the bathroom and wet one of the hand towels. *Best to not think about what else is cleaned up in this seedy motel on the side of the highway.*

Holding Mikki's knee, I tried to dab at the wound. The water soaked her dress into the wound, which caused Layla to glare. "Move this first," she said in nurse mode. I reached for Mikki's hemline and froze. The back of my neck burned as two women glared at me, waiting for me to undress the one I didn't want to.

"For fuck's sake," Mikki cursed. "I'll do it." She didn't just lift her dress, but grabbed the towel and took to wiping. "Ah! For all the sons of the moon and sun!" Her cursing shifted to her first language, tears beading in Mikki's eyes. Suddenly, her retracted wings burst from the ether. I watched with some satisfaction as one smacked Ink's face. He barely shifted at the attack, while poor Mikki's left wing crumpled.

"All right, witch of the realms. Do whatever you have to before I fucking pass out."

Layla pushed me aside so she could lean over the wound and draw her healing ward. The circle formed around Mikki's wound, but the final inside lines had to dart close. Without pause, Mikki reached for my arm. Her nails dug into my skin, embedding glitter and small rhinestones into me.

There was no doubt that Layla noticed, even as she kept administering aid to her patient. "All done," she declared, sitting back. The ward on Mikki's leg began to fade, the once wet black ink drying to an off-gray.

"Fuckity shit's snacks and the whole crapping market!" Mikki shouted. She raised her leg off the bed, her ankle pointed as she strained in what looked like agony.

Was it not working? I'd seen Layla's healing spell do amazing, damn near impossible things. I'd felt it myself. Even if the bullet remained in my thigh, the pain vanished in hours. Mikki hadn't taken the full spread, but enough buckshot was in her that it had to hurt.

"That is a goddamn trip!" Mikki shouted. "Whew! Feels like I'm coming off a full-on ambrosia high." She snapped her head, causing the last of her updo to fall apart. The purple half of her hair swung down to her shoulders, most of it stained from the dirt of Kansas as we'd run through the night. "I can see why you're keeping a witch for yourself. No one told me they could do that."

I put on a smile, hoping Layla would take that as an ego boost. Her magic had saved yet another life. But her frown deepened and she snapped her book shut. "So, wings. Are you a fairy?"

"Fuck no," Mikki snorted. "See me prancing around mucking about in people's love lives and turning them into armadillos for fun?" She shoved a hand to the bed and tried to sit up even with her healing leg extended. "I'm a nymph."

"A-a nymph? Like a, one of those." Layla swung her hands through the air and gave a half turn. "You're a... You carried a nymph, while naked?"

"She spent most of the time riding on my back," I said. I didn't need the flash of anger in Layla's eyes to tell me that wasn't the right thing to say. Just as long as she didn't ask me how I knew Mikki it should be fine. "Nymphs aren't...they're not whatever you're thinking."

"And what *am* I thinking?" Layla stepped in front of me. I locked my hands together and remembered I was still naked.

"That I'm a sexed-up tart running around banging anything that moves?" Mikki interrupted. "All lies, natch. Propaganda from those goat-blowing satyrs. I don't even have a boyfriend."

Layla's mouth dropped open, her eyes wide. I could see her wanting to say that didn't help. Okay, I could either wait for the truth to leak out or tell her now. "What matters is that she's safe. Right, Mikki?"

"I'd prefer living to being netted up by some jackasses in suits with their anuses sewn up in golden thread."

That finally caused Ink to rise from his observation chair. I gritted my teeth, but he asked, "Netted?" At least there wouldn't be any innuendo about knitting someone's ass together.

"Yeah." Mikki turned to him, and her dilated pupils shrunk to pinpricks. "Is that a fucking demon?"

"A sin of lust, if you please," Ink said with a deep bow.

"Shit. Everyone gives me the business for what I am and there you are screwing anything till the sun don't shine."

That brought a disconcerting chuckle from the demon. But I'd been around Ink long enough to know that if he was pressing on something, it mattered. "Mikki. What happened with those guys?" I turned to Layla to add, "She was surrounded when I found her. They shot her in the leg and the wing."

Tugging down her left wing, Mikki frowned at the glitter folding in on itself. "Don't suppose you got some magic drawing to fix this?"

Layla tried to reach out and trace a line, but the wing wasn't corporeal. Only the sparks existed for a brief second before fading away. She sighed and shook her head. "Sorry."

"Story of my life. Being trapped on this piece-of-shit earth ain't helping either. I can't feel crap." Mikki reached down and brushed her hand over the carpet, her face contorting in pain.

Fingers cupped my arm, pulling me until I found Layla staring down my leg. "You're covered in blood. Why don't I help you wash up so you can, ya know, not be naked anymore?"

Being a werewolf was as good as growing up in a nudity camp. Even puberty hadn't stopped my brothers and me from running around starkers at home all the time. I pulled in a sharp breath, foreign embarrassment striking me, and a scent of arousal tickled straight from my brain to my cock.

Shit. I tried to hide away the sudden rise with my palm, but Layla tugged me into the bathroom. The sound of her slamming the door and wordlessly drenching a bath towel in the sink deflated the rush of blood in an instant. I gritted my teeth, fearing she'd smack my leg with the wet towel. But as she dropped to a knee, she used tender passes to wipe away the crusted and fresh blood.

"Another bullet wound?" Layla whispered and I winced.

"Shotgun blast."

She shivered. "I hate having to heal them. I hate that I even need to know the difference. One's got bullets, I know, but a shotgun's—"

"Tiny beads crammed into a plastic casing. Causes a range of damage instead of a narrower strike of a bullet. There were a lot of guns around in the...you know," I muttered, my mood darkening. The last time she'd had to heal a bullet wound it was because the cult had put it there. And that night, I'd lost damn near my whole family.

"Who is she?" Layla asked in such a soft tone I barely heard it. Maybe she didn't even mean for me to, but werewolf ears.

"Mikki's a friend, an old friend from when I was a kid."

"You lived in Kansas for a time?" The blood was gone, but Layla kept dabbing the towel down my leg and wiping my feet.

"No. This was in Arizona. We tried, but there was the second pack. That's what doesn't make any sense. Mikki's a desert nymph. Sand, rock, sun. Those are her...domain? Nymph things? I don't know how it all works."

I'd been ten, doing a summer run through the desert. Not smart as a wolf, doubly not smart in the afternoon with the sun beating down. I'd tried crawling into the shadow of a rocked twisted into shape by the winds. And when I had shifted, suddenly there'd been Mikki, curious about a wolf who became a boy.

"Let me get this straight. You're called back home, and on the trip there, you just happen to come across an old friend who's miles from where she lives?" Layla said, rising from the ground to hang the drenched towel on the shower rack.

"What are you getting at?"

"None of that sounds suspicious? Or..." In the tiny bathroom there was nowhere for us to move. Layla stood beside the stained tub while I nearly had my ass on the counter. A movement of pink caused me to glance over my shoulder. The full wall of mirrors reflected my sorry state and the top of my buttocks squeezing against the Formica.

"Was that why you ran from me when we were almost, we'd been...? Huh?" she asked in a voice crackling with another question. I twisted around, forgetting the mirror and the copycat's back threaded with scars.

"Layla, hon, I..." What was the better answer? *Yes, I ran out on you in the middle of sex because I sensed my old friend in danger?* Did she want to hear that?

She bit her lip, hard. A line of white chased across the pink of her mouth, zapping me back to the moment when I'd had her against the wall. "I had no idea it was Mikki. I'd been running for, I dunno, an hour and I heard someone cry out."

My stomach clenched at the truth, knowing how bad that sounded. Her gaze drifted up to me, the question of why I ran lingering in there. I braced for it, but a single laugh shot from Layla. "Of course you did. Straight into danger without a second thought to save a stranger. Two guys, with guns?"

"To be fair, one was armed with a net-gun. Which I guess is a thing now."

Her shoulders lowered and her lips absently pushed together and opened. I stroked her cheek, uncertain what she'd do. Layla leaned closer, encouraging me. Without a moment's hesitation, I pulled her into my arms.

And when the strength of her body, the indomitable spirit of her mind and the tender touch of her fingers locked in my embrace, I shattered. I wanted to beg for her forgiveness, and I didn't even know why. Just to hear her say she understood, she'd absolve me. That I was good enough to be with her.

"Layla, I am..." My palms kept pushing back the baby hairs clinging to her forehead, my lips pressing against it. I couldn't get them to stop even if I wanted to. Two decades of a fucked-up psyche built behind that kiss, wanting to be unleashed in one go. I ran because we'd been running from the monster at the dinner table for as long as I could remember. *And even though he's dead, he won't leave.*

The tips of her fingers brushed my cheek as Layla wiped her eyes. "Can you just do something for me?"

Nodding, I dug my claws into the floor. *No, toes.* There were no claws.

"The next time you have to do the whole wolf thing, can you give me a little warning?"

She thought that I'd... I bounced my chin fast, trying to insist that I would give her a day's warning before I'd have to transform.

"Good, good, because it was—" Her nose crinkled like she didn't want to say how being abandoned felt. "A little weird to have Ink saunter in after."

"Did he, you two, um...?" Why was I asking that? I could smell the evidence all over her. Which didn't put the wolf off for one-second. Despite getting an opportunity to flex its fangs, it wanted me to shred her clothing and use the mirror to its full advantage.

A frown bunched Layla's face. She didn't shove me away, but her body slipped from mine. "What did you think would...? He's an incubus. It's like leaving out a cookie."

"You are not a dry-ass cookie. You're a cheesecake, with no cracks, smooth as cream and cherries on top." Rumbling rose in my gut, but as her cheeks blushed and her lashes fluttered, I couldn't say if I wanted cheesecake or *cheesecake*.

"That so?" Layla asked, defiantly lifting her head and meeting me eye to eye.

"A tiramisu. No, that dessert that rises, but you have to get it just right. Ah yes, a flan."

Her chuckle lifted my lips in a smile. She reached over to lightly slug me in the arm, the same way she had when I'd make a pun out of our study material. I caught her fist before it made contact. Layla's eyes opened in surprise, and I pulled her into my arms. Before she could say a word, I tipped her back over the tub and kissed her. She gripped the shower curtain, even though I had her safe.

Nip her throat. Run your palm over her breast. You can already feel her nipples straining against the tank top. Come on.

A knock at the bathroom door startled us both. I helped Layla back to her feet as a calm voice said, "If you've finished, the young nymph and I believed it prudent to acquire the wheel of cheese and bread."

Wheel of cheese and bread? I mouthed to Layla who laughed and sighed.

"He means pizza. We're coming, Ink."

"That is rather the point of it all," he muttered while walking away.

Layla adjusted her top, drawing my eyes to her dark nips straining the pink and blue fabric farther. She reached for the door, about to exit, when her eyes darted down to my crotch. "How about I get you your clothes? So you don't have to walk around...naked. Hm?"

"That, uh." I tried to cover myself by twisting to the side. It didn't help, my cock swinging from the momentum like a manic metronome. "That's a good idea."

With a sigh, she vanished from the bathroom. I hadn't told her everything about Mikki, but maybe it wouldn't matter. It felt like a lifetime ago.

Besides, Layla's too cool to care.

"Here," she said, and my jeans struck my face. "Your nymph wants pepperoni," was her parting comment before once against slamming the door.

Maybe not as cool as I thought. Simmering more like.

Chapter Twelve

Layla to my left, Mikki on the right and me awkwardly crammed in the middle of the bed. The demon kept drifting around the room like he had hemorrhoids, but that wasn't my problem. A single slice of pizza remained in the box, its plastic cheese adhering to the side. We'd fallen into a three-way stalemate, no one willing to risk crossing the border to take it.

"I like your hair," Layla said, patting at her dark brown locks.

"Oh?" Mikki sat up and instantly started combing down her mix of reds and purples. "Thanks. It grows out of my head even when I don't want it to."

"Manic Panic?"

The nymph frowned. "Manic what now?"

"The color. I was wondering if you got it from, it's so vibrant I thought maybe, ya know, the Manic Panic dye."

"Ah! You think it's fabricated. No, this is all natural," Mikki said, rapidly twisting her long hair into a braid while Layla shifted. I watched her fold her arms tighter to her chest and lock her legs in. That probably wasn't good.

"Though, by desert nymph standards, it's pretty boring. I mean, there's barely any orange and no yellow to speak of. You should see the river nymphs though. All they get is grunge gray and dirty mud. Maybe a touch of filthy blue for good measure. Ha!"

"I used to wear pink streaks, but they're just clip-ins. Haven't had much time to bother lately," Layla whispered, her eyes swinging to the spell book left on the bed. It currently held our complimentary array of napkins.

I began to reach for her, to run my hand down her back and tell her I liked her hair the way it was, when what Mikki said struck me. "Since when do you have anything to do with water nymphs?"

Mikki folded her nose so tight that her upper lip tucked back to give her a rodent look. She stopped pawing at her hair and began to rock on her side. "There's a...a reason why I'm traveling through this fucked-up state with dead dirt. I was an exchange."

An exchange? She looked at me as if I should know exactly how painful that was, but for the life of me, I had no clue.

"What's that mean?" Layla asked, stepping right into the conversation.

"Nymph society is always trading one child for another. It keeps their various factions 'out of war.'" Ink talked right over Mikki, causing the subject of that conversation to turn and glare at the pacing demon. "Am I incorrect?"

"Nah, the fuckstick has the right of it. I'd been 'in residence at the river queen's discretion' for the past... How old are you?"

I blinked at the question aimed at me, as if I could have anything to do with Mikki being shipped off across the country. "Twenty, twenty-seven."

"So, ten years. They never make trades until we're 'of age.' What's that face there, Claw?" Mikki waggled her finger over me, freezing whatever face I was making. "Oh, shit, nah. That trade came out of nowhere. Politics. We broke up for different reasons."

"Excuse me?" Layla sputtered, lunging forward and grabbing Mikki's hand with hers. The nymph's dark gaze drifted up to Layla, but she didn't fight back. "Cal, did she say broke up?"

"That..." *Fuck.* My whole body began to shrink. I tried to slide away, only for my back to smack into the headboard. There was nowhere to go and Layla was staring at me like a rattler watching a mouse limp over the sand.

"He was more pup than wolf back then. Dumbass kids playing in the dunes. Though, shit, were my sisters jealous."

"You should have seen my broth...I mean, ah, it was so long ago I, uh." My tongue dried out, my head swiveling from a smiling, unaware Mikki to the witch about to go nuclear.

"No, please continue," Layla said, her voice the final wind whistling through the coffin as it's lowered into the ground. "I believe you were going to say your brothers were jealous of your incredibly hot nymph girlfriend."

"You think I'm hot?" Mikki asked in surprise.

"Of course you are. For fuck's sake, you're a nymph. How can you not be hot?"

"I've known quite a few gargoyles in my day. Though, I guess when you're stuck embodying rock, there's not much you can do about it."

What if I slipped out of the window? Transformed into a wolf and kept running until daylight? It had to be hours off and surely Layla would cool off by then. My ears picked up the grinding of her molars and all my escape plans vanished. "Mikki is a friend..." I said, my lips wide in a painful smile I'd hoped would diffuse the situation.

"Who was once your girlfriend. See, that's easy."

"As easy as you saying, 'This is my incubus. He's part of the package deal.'"

Layla jabbed her finger at me. "Hey, I told you about him."

"Only when I appeared after their first coitus attempt," Ink interjected.

Both Layla and I growled at him, "Stay out of this!"

"Very well, but this drama is far more delicious than the bland overtures on your phone," he huffed, sinking into the chair.

The smell of lightning right on the edge of a storm rose from Layla. I watched her, expecting sparks to fly from her fingertips or a deadly orb to begin spinning around her. But all she did was glare, her face darkening to a ruddy pink the longer she huffed.

"Oookay," Mikki declared. She twisted off the bed, landing on both feet without a single complaint. "I can see I kicked up an imp's nest here and do not want to have my name dragged up in any therapist sessions. So how about I...?" She made it three steps before her healing leg bounced against the bed. Glitter burst into the room from her wings unfurling only for the broken left to crumple, sending Mikki crashing to the ground.

I reached for her, but it was Layla who caught her arm. Not with her hands—she was too far away, but an invisible force burst from her palm and pinned Mikki up.

"Wait, that's dumb," Layla said. She scooted across the bed, dragging the comforter with her, to land on her bare feet in front of Mikki. "There's men in suits out there chasing you. Why are they chasing you?"

"Fuck if I know. Not the first time some forceless wonder got it in his head to come after a nymph. Though usually it's a witch or two hoping to restock her pantry."

Mikki's pupils slammed to slits thin as a pin. She stared at Layla, who hunched into her shoulders and looked at the bored demon. "I don't do that."

"Obviously. You're in your pajamas and they wore suits. Are we done?"

"Mik." Reaching for her, I caught her hand before she stormed out in a fit of lone wolf syndrome. The hair on the back of my neck stood on end as a warning, but I didn't let go. "Your wing's broken, your leg's still healing. Where do you think you're gonna go?"

"Home. For fuck's sake, Claw. That's where I've been trying to go since the Missouri nymphs sent me packing."

"They let you go? I thought the whole point of the trade was..."

Mikki sighed and shook her head. A rainbow of reds and purples momentarily sliced through the air. "Yes, yes, stop war. Keep all us fairy folk, not technically a fairy thank you, in check. So we don't rip open some stupid realm shit or whatever. But they said I was free to go. Get away from all that muck and flies. So many hivefucking flies. And my feet. You see my toenails? They ain't been clean in six years."

Slamming her hands together as if in prayer, though it was an old fae trick the humans mimicked, Mikki pulled in a breath. Her face shifted. The hard lines emphasizing her nose and cheeks faded, and in a softer tone she said, "I need to get home. They know I'm coming. And I'd like to feel proper sand under my feet before I go stark raving mad, thanks."

"If your collective knows you're coming, and you don't return…"

She tipped her head to the side. "Then it'll be war. Which will pit river against desert, and we all know how that one turns out."

Floods. Droughts. Famine either way. Entire ecosystems stripped of resources as the nymphs raged until one side was decimated. I'd only heard tales from Mikki and her other friends, but it sounded like when nymphs took up a cause, mass extinctions followed.

I had to get her home, not just for the whole world's sake, but for Mikki's too. I opened my mouth, about to say as much, when Layla spoke. "Then we'll take you," she said.

A chortle passed Mikki's lips, her head twisting from me to Layla. "Is that…are you? Wait, is this a sex thing?"

"What?"

"Like, drag me in the middle, get all steamed up in anger, scream at each other and boom!"

Ink snorted from the chair. "I wish."

"Will you keep—" Layla started, glaring at the insouciant demon.

I cupped a hand around Layla's shoulders, and she didn't shrug me off. "You don't have to do this," I whispered.

"Yes, we do. Look, I don't know what all entails a fairy war...sorry, nymph battle. But I'm guessing it's not good." Worried, she looked from me to Mikki, who gave a long whistle that ended with a boom and hand-mimed explosion. "She's injured, can barely walk or fly. And..." Layla swallowed deep, her gaze shifting away. "She's your friend. We should help her."

A bright spot wrapped through me at her tender plea. I reached to embrace Layla, her head almost landing on my shoulder, when the demon sprung from his chair. "Now that that matter is settled, shall we engage in an orgy? Nymph?"

Mikki's discerning eye shot down Ink. "That'll be a hard pass, demon. But I could use something to sleep in other than my bloody dress."

"I've got a shirt you can use," Layla said. She dug into her bag just as Mikki yanked her clothes off. Shit. I forgot that nymphs didn't do underwear. And I'd needed to turn around five seconds ago. My skin blistered while I felt the withering glare of Layla as she passed Mikki the top.

A hand pressed to my back, almost sending me into the air. "It's safe to look," Layla whispered in my ear.

I twisted around to her warm eyes and a hint of a smile on her lips. Thank the moon minions she found that hilarious. Tucking my thumb under her chin, I pulled her to me for a kiss of gratitude.

"Any chance you have something smaller? I'm swimming in this!"

My witch growled against my skin. "No," she spat fast, turning away from the half-dressed nymph who was drowning in a yellow T-shirt.

"Werewolf?" Ink called to me. The girls were gathering up the trash, obviously trying to look away the second the other was caught staring. It left me in the demon's sights. "Why don't we finally work through that tension in the room?"

"Ink," Layla sneered. "Drop it."

With a belabored sigh, the demon plummeted to his chair. "Very well. I know you're more than satisfied tonight, my bond."

And just like that, a massive ring of tension rose among everyone. My scalp prickled in a nervous energy I couldn't escape. Layla darted her gaze from me to Ink, then back to Mikki who was keeping a watch on all of us. Only Ink, the damn demon of hell, cared nothing for the mess he had started.

Picking up Layla's phone, Ink asked, "So who gets the bed?"

* * * *

Punching the solitary flat pillow, I curled onto my side and faced the dresser. A handful of golden sparkles kept erupting from the bed where Mikki slept beside Layla, the nymph's snoring distracting to two senses. Giving the bed to the two women had seemed the best answer, one I didn't think anything of until I realized I was stuck on the floor. And in the direct line of the glare off Layla's phone.

"Would it kill you to turn that off?" I asked, trying to whisper without waking the girls.

The demon crooked his head, his eyes glowing in the darkened room like candles in a crypt. "Doubtful, unless this Tube of You is cursed."

A sigh built deep in the back of my aching skull. He always played stupid when it suited him. I hurled myself to the ground, prepared to yank the blanket over my head, when a thought bounced around.

"Layla," I said, whispering to the dark. "You say you answer to her every desire."

"Not every. I'm in no mood to act as butler to her whims. But the ones that involve the vigorous rubbing of body parts, yes."

I watched the flicker of his reflection in the fake wood of the dresser's leg. He kept me under observation, as if he too wasn't certain what to make of this. "But you have to do everything she tells you to. No matter what."

"Ha. I'm afraid our dear does not seem to ache for the dominant life. Though there have been flitting thoughts involving leather straps at times."

That...actually, that didn't surprise me. She'd half joked about me wearing the collar from when I'd kept myself chained in the basement. And was even curious to see it on. Hm.

"But to answer your impolite question, no, I am free to refuse any request she makes of me. And she has the same. I dare say I am more bound to a code of proper conduct than even you."

"What?" I spun in place, twisting the flimsy, pilling blanket around my legs. "Are you, a fucking demon of all things, accusing me of—" I was so mad I couldn't even think it much less say the word.

"Merely pointing out a truth. By my nature I am bound to, shall we say, obey her desires whichever way they fall."

"So if she, in the middle of *being* with you, suddenly lost all interest...?"

"I would extract myself and find other entertainment. I've been watching many of these hacks of life. There is much use to be found from hot glue."

My stomach knotted at the thought. The sin of lust shook off Layla growing cold like it was nothing more than a minor cramp. Meanwhile, I couldn't stop picking at the damn thought. So she'd chosen him once. How many times had she abandoned Ink for me?

And there was no fucking way I could ask her that without everything falling to pieces.

"If I may offer a nibble of advice," the demon said, rising from his chair. He picked up the ice bucket, which he'd been eating out of all night. "No other man, woman or lover in the equation matters, as long as you are in control."

It sounded like he was trying to be sincere, as if he didn't want this tenuous relationship to snap apart. But I shook my head, none of it making sense. "In control of what?" I asked.

Ink paused beside the door, his chin cocking to the right. "Yourself," was his final word before he vanished to raid the ice machine for the third time.

I fumbled back to my makeshift bed. What was he talking about? I had complete control over myself. "Fucking demons," I muttered, biting into my pillow to soothe the ache in my clenching jaw.

* * * *

Take it.

"No. I don't want it."

But it's yours, Calvin. Take it.

I tossed my head, muddied hair smacking into my cheeks. My fingers clung together refusing to budge even as a force pried on them.

You are to take it.

A crowbar slipped between my palms, the cold metal cutting into my skin. I bit my lip, fighting down the cry of pain while the force pulled harder on my hands. But still they wouldn't come apart.

If you do not take it…

A whip cracked the air and a cry answered it. My heart stopped and I screamed, "Eli!"

Take it or he will suffer.

Without pause, I opened my hands. Heavy plastic, black as night, forced itself between my palms. On instinct, I clamped down, taking the full weight of the gun in my arms.

There. Eyes frozen solid stared at me, the face framed in white. *Accept what I give you, worthless cretin. If you don't…*

The whip cracked again and I cried in pain.

A hand slipped around my stomach. I opened my arms, casting the AR-15 to the ground. Spinning. My body inverted, the floor twisting in a vortex. I landed hard without falling an inch. *Pillow, blanket.* It was another dream.

And the hand?

Warmth radiated up my back and I spun my head around. For a moment I thought I saw the asshole, his lips soaked in beer, his fist bloody. But the clenching fear faded to reveal dark spirals brushing against my arm.

"Layla?" I sputtered, my heart pounding harder. The wolf wanted to run and I was tempted to join it.

She caressed her palm up my chest, her fingers landing right over my heart. "You were whimpering," she said, her voice drowsy.

Oh. I'd woken her. *Damn it.* "It was a…a nightmare. I'm sorry."

Tickling the back of my neck with her lips, Layla pulled more of her body around mine. I rested back into her arms, the urge to flee fading to a whisper.

"It's okay," she said.

I reached to cup her fingers, to thread my hand with hers and hold her with me. But that was selfish. "I'll be fine. You should head back to bed. The floor's not comfy."

Her gentle, soothing breath brushed down my neck. I expected her to slip away, maybe give me a single hug before she returned to the mattress. But Layla said, "If it's all the same, I'd rather stay here."

"Oh?"

The beat of her heart slowed mine, calmed it until the panicking ache washed from my limbs. Layla adjusted herself, causing her hair to tickle my cheek. From half-awake lips, she mumbled, "I sleep better with you."

"Then…" Swallowing down a knot I couldn't explain, I locked my fingers over hers. Resting deeper in her embrace, I whispered, "Stay."

Chapter Thirteen

Every bone in my body, even the ones that only formed when I went wolf, ached. My muscles shrieked like a petulant toddler mid-tantrum and no amount of carb-loaded chocolate bars would silence them. It was a pretty typical response to a night in a strange hotel room.

"Is that everything?" I asked automatically while placing Layla's bag in the trunk.

She paused, her lips pressed to a complimentary Danish that came in cellophane. Before I slammed the trunk closed, I said, "Did you check under the bed? Sometimes things can, um, ya know…"

Her mouth twitched up as if she were trying to fight a smile and my stomach burned hotter. Yeah, I knew how that made me sound like the old dad. But Mark was always forgetting shit in the bathroom, and we had to keep Eli from… *Damn it.* I smacked my palm to my eye socket, trying to shock the tears away.

Slipping close, Layla rested her head on my shoulder and asked softly, "Are you okay?" Despite having lain beside me on the floor until dawn, she was beautiful. Bright and joyful, even before her coffee.

I wrapped my hands around hers, trying to squeeze assurance that I was fine. Just grief being the clingy bastard it always was. Trying to not think about Eli didn't work. I'd shatter into smaller pieces. "Long night," I said instead.

Her gaze narrowed, Layla knowing I held something back, but it was Mikki who spoke up. "Tell me about it." She'd knotted the borrowed shirt at the bottom so it revealed her midriff and slipped on a pair of Layla's biker shorts. It left Mikki looking like a lost college kid on spring break while we tried to not shiver against the rotten winter winds.

"Your hair?" Layla asked, pointing to the now dishwater blonde locks Mikki piled into a lazy bun.

"Didn't want to startle any mortals lurking about so I toned it down. Am I adequately bland?" She perched on a single tiptoe and raised her back leg up like an anime character.

"It's…" I began when an ancient instinct long passed down the werewolf line warned me. "Fine," I finished, turning away without glancing at her. After slamming the trunk closed, I lingered while Layla asked Mikki about her leg. The wing was a bigger problem.

"We ready to head out?" I asked, looking at both women.

"Hmph." Ink emerged from the lobby with two donuts in each hand. "They refused to let me bring a fresh bucket of ice with me."

"You can't take an ice bucket, not without buying it," Layla muttered.

The demon paused, his head tilting while he crammed all the donuts into one palm. "I offered to hold the ice in my pockets," he said and shoved four donuts into his mouth at once. *How did anyone find that attractive?*

"They'd fucking melt," Layla scolded him, rolling her eyes so I'd laugh.

By the powers of hell, not a single crumb escaped from Ink's masticating jaws. "Exactly. There's much interesting fun to be had with a single." He bounced the tip of his pinkie against Layla's nose. "Cube." The next finger touched the top of her lips. "Of ice," he purred, curling the whole of his sticky hand around her jaw.

That man was exhausting. I glared at my shoes, trying to ignore the incubus's need to always be the center of attention. "Why don't I drive?" I shouted. "Take the long stretch? I mean, you did it all yesterday."

Layla pursed her lips. "Are you sure you're not...too tired?"

"I'm good," I tried to assure her. Driving was good for me. Forced to focus on the tick of speedometer, the pass of the yellow lines, the rise and fall of traffic, my mind couldn't churn apart my mess of a life. I just wished my jaw would stop aching.

"Okay," she said, and tossed me the keys. I dropped my hand from rubbing my cheek and caught them. A metal keychain of a kitten in a witch's hat swung free, and I smiled. I'd gotten it for her for Christmas. We'd both agreed that the best gift after a long shift on Christmas Eve were his and hers foot rubs. But I'd spotted it and couldn't help myself.

Her soft lips parted in a smile. *Leap over the car, slide across its hood, take her in your arms, and kiss her until the frosty air melts on her cheeks.*

"I call shotgun!" Mikki shouted, slipping into the front seat before anyone could blink.

Layla's gaze darted to Ink, who smiled like the pig that found the hallucinogenic mushrooms. *Great.* Placing on a smile that knotted a node of tension in my skull, I dropped into the driver's seat. My knees were practically in my stomach. *Have to adjust that.*

"Hey," Ink shouted as I shoved the car's seat back to make room. His fingers curled around the headrest and he pulled himself closer. "If you wanted to sit in my lap, you only had to ask."

Yanking on the control, I eased the driver seat forward. Layla knocked into Ink's arm, the two whispering in an obvious fight. There it went again.

"Very well," the demon declared. "I will simply keep my legs upon my bond." He twisted in his seat, resting half of his body on Layla's lap. With a shake of her head, she turned to stare out of the window, but I watched her hand gently caress up and down Ink's gangly legs.

Another ten hours to go. I flipped on the first radio station I found. Fire and brimstone preaching about the immorality of sex outside of marriage blasted through the car. With a groan, I merged into traffic, not bothering to change the station.

* * * *

Kansas would never end.

In theory, it was only an hour to the border, but as I stared across the landscape straining to the horizon without a break in sight, I knew I'd never make it. The state would swallow me whole until only a car with no passengers inside rolled into Oklahoma.

"Cal?" I jerked upright, slamming my knee into the car door and squeezing harder on the gas pump handle. Swallowing the gnarl of pain radiating down my leg, I turned to Layla who'd slipped out of the backseat along with everyone else to stretch her legs. "You okay?"

"Yep." I nodded vehemently, hoping that'd provide a jolt of energy to my system. The morning rolled into an afternoon with me sitting on the edge of my seat waiting for either Mikki or Ink to plunge the four of us into a civil war. They'd actually been relatively quiet— only a minor argument had broken out about fairy dust. But the stress of it punched harder into the back of my skull than a cult-enforcer's boot.

Layla's concerned smile drooped. "Are you sure about that? Because you're not pumping out any gas." She jabbed to the digital numbers that remained on zero across the board.

"Damn it!" I lifted out the hose then rammed it back in, causing the car to shake on its axles.

"Gentle, wolf," the demon called, stretching his arms wide. One just had to land across Layla's shoulders, didn't it? "We don't want to rupture our chariot's combustion orifice. Not without picking a safe word, at least."

Layla's exasperated sigh rattled through me, causing me to stare down at the plugged gas nozzle. "It must be broken," I muttered, abandoning any pretense of the gasoline starting to flow on its own. Lifting the nozzle free, with one hand under to catch any potential drips, I paused at Ink's leer. Why did he have to enjoy everything so much? Would it kill him to have one bad day?

"I'll pull the car around to another…" I began, when I noticed the switch on the pump was down. Of course it was. A thousand curses birthed and died on my tongue. Too exhausted to scream a single one, I only let out a grunting groan while flipping the switch up and returning the nozzle. Now the numbers and gas were flowing.

Ink turned to the pump's display and smiled. "A gentle hand can make all the difference in the world."

"Will you…?" Layla began, her voice cold, when she skirted over to the disheveled lump struggling to display a modicum of masculinity for her. "Head inside, Ink. There's snacks."

"Wonderful. I assume the wolf requires more of his Whodunnits for the trip?" he asked no one but the air. In truth, he was right. I'd torn through almost my entire stash and restocking was necessary before my next shift. But my ears had already blanked out the demon, and I only heard Layla because she glanced a hand over my back.

"You look exhausted," she said, digging the heel of her palm into my shoulders to try and remove the knots. I'd probably need her walking on my back to pop them free. And the demon too.

"It's this fucking state," I said too loudly, making people who drove vehicles with Kansas license plates look my way. *Oops.* "I'm just…I want to get to my mom. Make sure she's okay."

"Did you hear from her?"

"A quick text. Which is not like her. Though she also sent me an image of a turtle eating a strawberry, so maybe I'm overreacting." The nymph, incubus and witch issue were the least of my problems. But if I wasn't worrying about Layla growing angry over Mikki, I had my mother in the path of a pack of werewolves to freak out over. Even trying to focus on home left me with another semester of nursing school, my brain-numbing job or the six-foot-deep hole where my brother lay. Nothing was working.

Layla brushed her cheek to mine, the movement soothing back the hackles I didn't realize were up. "We'll get there, I promise. My car hasn't let me down yet." She patted the roof with affection.

"My bond!" Ink shouted from directly outside the door into the cramped convenience store. "I found the perfect adornment for your chariot!" He hoisted up a bumper sticker that said *My other ride is a broom* and had a silhouette of a witch on it.

Rubbing her temples, Layla ran to Ink and started to shove him back inside. "I swear to god…" she said, before her words were cut off by the *bing-bong* of the store's door.

Numb, I watched the gallon meter roll up, hitting fifteen and continuing past. Layla said her tank held sixteen. I should have stopped earlier. *For lunch. Let us all take a breather.* But the longer we were all together, the higher the chances of the tenuous ceasefire erupting increased. I couldn't escape the certainty I was sitting on a powder keg I really didn't want to blow.

After checking twice that I'd closed the gas tank door and hung up the nozzle, I stood before the car. I should take a piss. My werewolf bladder let me hold it longer than the average human, but it wasn't smart to risk stones for the sake of getting home five minutes early. As I stared through the glass windows of the store, watching Layla first playfully smack Ink on the chest then pull him to her for a kiss, I lost all nerve.

Crunching over the scattered gravel, my shoes led me past the parking lot and down the ditch. A massive boulder was propped up beside the wooden sign for gas and food. Mikki's bare feet kept her pinned to the top of the giant rock, her toes dancing around like they were playing the piano.

"Well, well," she said, twisting her head to me. I stared in confusion at the bland ashy brown hair, not used to it. The lack of purples and reds made her look like an entirely different girl. "Look at what the cat dragged in. You look like shit."

There was that heart-stabbing honesty I always expected from Mikki. Shoving my hands under my arms for warmth, I tried to ignore the cold rattling across the plains. A dusting of gray snow lingered over the ground, one that'd hopefully vanish as we kept heading south.

"I hate this state," I said honestly.

Mikki raised her hand, causing a sprinkling of dirt to float into the air. "Tell me about it." She sighed, then dropped her hand to me. "Come on up."

I took it, following her to perch upon the boulder. My left leg dangled to the side and I crooked my right to keep me safe on top. Mikki managed to keep herself pinned even with half her body floating in air. Nymphs didn't go in much for gravity.

Shaking her head, Mikki leaned back and cursed, "Nothing's fucking right here. All I want is to get home. Is that too much to ask for?"

With a shrug, I was about to tip back and join her staring into the vast gray sky. What we both wanted instead of brown ditches and dishwater clouds was a sea of red stretched before us and dunes swelling from the wind's commands. A sky bluer than any ocean, the clouds forever puffed up like a jack rabbit's tail. We wanted home.

I flinched at the idea and froze before lying down beside Mikki. School wasn't in Santa Fe. Layla wasn't there either. "Being trapped with the river nymphs...it must have been awful," I said.

Mikki shifted her head on the boulder, her eyes shut tight. "I shouldn't complain so fucking much. It'll give me wrinkles. I wasn't locked in a cage and fed only bread and water. No queen in her right mind would treat an exchange that way."

"But to be cut off from your friends, your family, for...years." It sounded horrible. To be nothing more than a political pawn tossed from one side to the other in order to keep peace.

But Mikki took it all with another shrug. Bundling her hands under her head, she said, "I dunno. I couldn't stand half of my collective anyway. What about you? How are your brothers getting on? Mark still a raging asshole about the world?"

Thunder clapped in my heart. On a good day, Mikki was completely oblivious to her words stinging. When she sat up and stared at me, I knew I must've looked more like death than even she'd say. "Something...happened," I whispered, knotting my fingers together.

My fists started to shake, my nails flexing against the rising bones in my hands. "Eli's, he's..." I dug in, the pain in my jaw throbbing. In one fast go, I said, "The asshole killed him."

"Fucking hell!" Mikki exclaimed. "Is he coming after you?" She sprang up from her sunbathing, her head whipping around.

"No." I tried to shake my head, but I could only manage a half turn. My neck twisted like a malfunctioning robot. "We got him. We finally put him in the fucking ground."

Cold, quiet earth where no one would bother him except the deer and roots from the summer trees. Eli had liked it there, the only spot where we'd felt we weren't tools for the cult.

A hand smacked into my back, startling me. I slammed my hands to the rock. Stinging rose from my palms and I flinched, realizing I'd shifted my claws. *Damn it.* I tried to stuff my hands away, but Mikki leaned closer to my face.

"Good. That's good, right?"

"Yeah," I nodded. "It's a good thing."

"Which one of you did the deed?"

Me. I did. I plunged my teeth into the throat of the man who'd terrorized us all our lives. Who beat Eli because he wasn't strong like Mark, because he wasn't me.

"Mark," slipped from my lips. *The lie.* The one I had to keep repeating until I believed it. I twisted from Mikki, certain she'd pick up on it. *Drill me.* Get me to confess that I couldn't escape the taste of my father's blood or the crick in my jaw from where my back teeth had scissored his trachea.

She laughed. "Figures. He always did go on and on about being the one to end it. No offense, but your brother's a two-headed rattlesnake." I'd probably have said the same, chuckled at Mikki's description, but I couldn't get the stench of diesel fuel, gun oil and salted pork out of my nose.

"Sorry though, that it took Eli to do it." Mikki tipped her head down in mourning, before popping up with a big smile. "At least you don't have to worry about that prophecy anymore."

"Yeah…" I rocked on my tailbone digging into the boulder.

"I always thought that lady was full of it anyway. 'Whosoever destroys the alpha will take the pack as his own.' Psh. Fortunetellers just tell you what you want to hear. She probably meant it for Mark. Bet if we found her today, she'd say the spirits were trying to reach him instead. Woo."

Destroy the alpha, take over the pack.

Usurp the father, become the monster in the mirror.

That was what he'd wanted, what he screamed at us for. The three true werewolves, born of his blood. Mark had been strong and belligerent, the firstborn. It should have been him. But I'd come a year later, with his hair, his face. It had been me he'd wanted to fill the role. To be the enforcer and lieutenant when I grew up.

Poor Eli. He hadn't asked to be born last. To have been soft spoken, and tender. To have earned the wrath of the man who only cared about strength and cruelty just for daring to be quiet and kind and look like him.

I yanked on my hair, wishing it'd all fall out. A clean slate. No more catching my reflection in the mirror and my heart stopping because it had learned the blond man was a threat. But it didn't work. It had never worked. Dyeing it didn't help. A shift that night would erase it back to blond. I could never be rid of him because no matter what I did, he'd always be half of me.

The half that had murdered his father without a second thought.

"Caly?" Mikki asked. She draped a hand over my shoulders and leaned in closer. "What's wrong?"

"Are you ready to go?"

Shit. I spun around to find Layla standing behind us. Her face was unreadable, but I knew whatever she was feeling couldn't be good.

Without pause, I hurled myself off the boulder. My ankle fumbled in the dirt, but I kept going, dashing to stand beside Layla. My heart pounded, a fear rising through me that I couldn't name. She stared at Mikki and only flicked her gaze to me for a second. But then Layla turned, her mouth parting as she laid a hand to my chest.

My head fell, unable to summon the energy to tell her what she was about to ask. I felt her fingers crest against my cheek, but still I wouldn't look up. "Why don't I take over driving? You could catch a nap in the back."

Curling my palm around her wrist, I dragged Layla's fingertips to my lips. Not for a kiss, just a reminder that she was here and not some fevered mirage from my dying mind. "Okay," I whispered and moved to hand her the keys.

Layla refused. "You should get in the back now. Lie down before you fall down. That's an order from a student two semesters away from being an RN."

I laughed, my voice strained in exhaustion. "I will," I said, then glanced at Mikki, who was still perched on the rock.

Following my look, Layla said, "I was going to check on her leg. See if it needs any healing. We'll meet you back at the car."

My weary body turned, the promise of sleep—even if it was crammed in the backseat—calling it home.

"Oh," Layla said to me, "Ink found one of those bikini T-shirts and refuses to take it off, so have fun with that."

Before I could even understand that jumbled image, Layla stepped over to Mikki. "How's the leg?" It wasn't a warm request by any means, but I couldn't say it was cold either.

Growing aware of the women watching me, I started to shuffle to the car, but my ears homed in on them. Even when I reached the parking lot, I could hear every word.

"Honestly, it feels good as new," Mikki said. "The wing I'm more worried about."

"Don't take it out here," Layla responded quickly.

"I wasn't gonna. Shit, I've probably been blending in as human longer that you've been born. You're like eighteen, right?"

What the hell was that, Mikki?

Layla gave a non-committal chortle. Not a laugh, but not a growl either. "That how you know Cal? You were blending in at his school?"

"Nah. He was... Can I ask you something?" Mikki turned on a dime. Layla must have nodded as she continued, "Does he...?"

Oh god, Mikki! How bad was this going to be? Sex stuff? The asshole's death? Probably sex stuff.

"Does he shift?"

Crap.

"Yeah. Every night. Why?" Layla went from earnest to detective on the scent in a second.

"Just that, when we were kids he once went a whole month without shifting."

"What happened?"

My stomach twisted into a pretzel of shame. I clung to my belly, fiddling with the rows of abs growing stronger from every full moon.

"They ain't supposed to do that, I guess. Not shifting is bad news. Cal, the wolf in him, it rebelled. He ran off into the desert for a week. Nobody could find him. By the time they did, he was half starved and suffering heat stroke."

"Jesus!"

"Just, watch him. Okay. I'll never forget that look on his face when he shifted back after so long as the wolf. And I'm starting to see it again."

I wanted it gone, all of it. The hair, the eyes, the wolf always prowling in my head. But it didn't work. Every time I tried to wipe it away, it just came back stronger.

The wolf wasn't happy with how the asshole had ended. It had wanted him to suffer. To know every torturous day he'd put us through. But Lucien was gone, and I had no idea how to appease the bloodthirsty monster inside me.

Chapter Fourteen

"Oh, that's adorable."

Layla's voice sounded about to both laugh and squee as I woke. I pinched into my eyes, refusing to lift the lids. My neck ached from the inhumane angle I'd crooked it into, but at least I'd finally passed out on the other side of the demon.

"That's nothing. You should see him on his skateboard."

Skateboard? How...? *Oh, shit!*

I sprang up so fast the child safety locks clicked on. The seatbelt strap dug into my neck, trying to pin me into place and a gulping "oof" escaped my lips. "What are you looking at?" I shouted even with my brain filling in the pieces.

The demon clicked his claws. "You in your adolescent stage. I believe attempting to pilot a wagon-less cart off a staircase."

Damn it, Mikki. She held a red crystal in her hands, an image of me at eleven projected five inches above it.

I tried to reach forward to run my hand through it and shake the image away, but the damn seatbelt locked tighter.

"I can't believe that's you, any of you," Layla said, her voice bubbling in laughter.

My leg started to shake, the nervous embarrassment twisting to an anger I couldn't get out. Of course she'd find it funny. Werewolves were notorious for carrying puppy fat as kids. A lot of it. It hadn't been enough to be the weirdoes who'd come to school in ripped clothing and couldn't sit still. We'd all been chunky to the point that it was all they'd taunt us over...until Mark had tried to break one kid's arm. That had stopped it fast. And we'd had to move again.

"I can explain," I said, my brain filling with physiological stats I'd read on the werewolf dark web. *Once puberty hits, the werewolf metabolism shifts into overdrive. All that fat stored in childhood is used to aid in proper shifts, which requires the consumption of a near constant state of protein and carbs.*

Layla's gaze danced up to the rearview mirror. I read only delight in her eyes, causing me to stare down at my feet. "Really? You can explain the triple bowl cuts?"

"That..." My excuses all slammed into a wall. She was laughing at our hair. "Uh, no. I guess they were considered cool in Utah?"

Mikki scrolled through the old images she took of us. They were grainy and washed out, but I recognized me standing lookout while Mark had tried to knock sodas loose from a machine. And there was Eli at the waterpark, in full floaty wings and a life jacket. He'd hated the water so much, he'd never learned how to swim.

And never would.

"You appear perturbed," Ink said. His eyes crawled over me, but I didn't have the strength to face him for another round. "Would you like to rest upon my shoulder?" He patted the body part on offer and smiled.

A flash of anger burned from the rearview mirror straight to the incubus. But Ink paid no attention to Layla's obvious command to lay off. My stomach twisted at the rising tension and I grabbed the door handle out of habit, as if leaping out going sixty was a good idea.

"Where are we?" I asked, hoping to change the topic of conversation.

"Almost out of Oklahoma," Layla answered.

Damn, I went down that long? Last I remembered, we were still an hour to get out of Kansas, and here came New Mexico. Honestly, the landscape didn't look that different. The horizon stretched in an unwavering plane far beyond what even I could see. Brown and red dirt, dotted with a sprinkling of white snow from a passing storm could belong to any of the neighboring states. But, as I pulled in a breath of air recycled through the car's heater, I smelled home. And also a mass of moths stuck to the car's grill.

"How are we all...um, how's it going?" I asked, realizing I'd left Layla alone with Mikki for hours.

The nymph kept flicking through her crystal, highlighting old images from the desert proper. There was one from when I'd posed with the Montezuma Castle in the background. While the tourists had hiked around the edge, we'd snuck up inside to find an elf tear hidden right behind the walls. Which was around the time I'd first kissed Mikki, first kissed a girl.

Unbuckling my seatbelt, I dashed for the front of the car and clasped my hand over the crystal. The image I knew was coming up collapsed back into the ether of magic. "Hey," Mikki complained.

"Cal, what are you doing?" Layla scolded.

"I just...I didn't want you..." To have to see my sad case of young infatuation. To start yet another argument when we already had so many simmering in back.

"Buckle your ass up," Layla thundered, swiveling her head to me. I froze at the rising anger in her voice and the red burning over her cheeks. Did she know why? Could she sense it, or had Mikki already told her?

"I'll..." I drifted from her to the road. "Look out!"

Layla whipped her gaze and immediately slammed on the brakes. Everyone still locked in by their seatbelts rocked to the strain of the nylon strap. Meanwhile, my chin met with Mikki's headrest. Hard. *Fuck!*

Blood dripped down the back of my throat. I tipped my head back, certain more would gurgle from my nose and I tried to suck in a groan.

"What the— Is everyone all right?" Layla called, the car squealing to a stop inches before it plowed into the bumper of an SUV frozen on the highway. A round of murmurs broke from the assembled crew, but Layla focused on me. "Cal?"

"Yeah. Shit!" I hissed, touching my chin. Pain snapped from that point back through my jaw. I watched the 'I told you so' wash over Layla's face, though she didn't say it. Sheepishly, I tugged the seatbelt down and clicked it into place.

"Here," the demon said, extending a handkerchief with an *M* monogram to me. I took it just as I felt the warm liquid burble from my nostril.

Silence reverberated in the vehicle, my legs tensing from the burst of adrenaline of the near miss. I could see Layla's hands shaking as she clung to the steering wheel. The close call didn't vanish into the air, but hung on, growing fatter the longer we sat in place. No one moved down the road.

I leaned against the window, my cheek plastered to the glass, as I stared up a straight line of cars evaporating into the horizon. Whatever had us stopped up was at least a mile away. *Great.*

We tried to play it cool for a few minutes. Layla fumbled through the radio, finding nothing worth listening to in broadcast range. Unsurprising — we were deep into country territory. She offered to let me stream through her car, but my phone was nearly dead and Ink wouldn't give up his nonstop entertainment.

The SUV moved two car lengths ahead, filling us with excitement that whatever roadblock had occurred had now cleared…only for us to stop a single fence post past where we'd been and begin the wait anew.

"This is fucking ridiculous," Layla snarled, slamming her palm to the wheel. "Does this happen a lot?"

Mikki shrugged. "I ain't been this far out since they shipped me away. Cal?"

I shook my head, trying to remember. Trips home had been very far and few between. But I couldn't remember ever being clogged on this highway pinched between open farmland. A tingle grew down my spine. I absently reached behind my neck to find all the hairs standing up.

"I wish I could see what's up there," Layla said, shifting in her seat to try to stand up in the car. "Wait. Ink?"

"Waiting, my bond," he said, the smugness radiating a full three-sixty.

"Can you do that whatever you do and see what's got us blocked?"

Laying his borrowed phone down on the seat between us, Ink said. "Of course. Be back in a tick." The air that'd held the incubus suddenly deflated. His seatbelt, uncertain about the lack of a man to pin in place, retracted like a whip. I shivered from the sound, and tried to focus on whatever he'd been doing with Layla's phone.

"Sheep wars?" I whispered to myself, when black hair smacked into my face.

Ink appeared perched in the middle of the car, his ass on the phone, fingers tented and digging into his spread-apart knees.

"Well?" Layla prompted. "What is it?"

"I didn't see," Ink said. He shook his head from one side to the next and flames climbed over his sclera.

Layla must not have seen how agitated the incubus was. "What the shit? You said you were going to look."

"Yes. I attempted to," he answered slowly, his jaw clenched so tight that small spikes erupted from the sides. That couldn't be good. "But I was incapable of getting near enough to see."

"Why? You can go anywhere. You do go anywhere you want." She was arguing with Ink, but it sounded more like her beef was with the universe.

If the demon couldn't get up there... *Oh shit. No.* They were a legend. A bogeyman told to children to keep them inline.

"The only thing capable of keeping a demon out is a ward of a witch," Ink said softly. Then his skin crackled, fire streaming from the gaps of the charred flesh as he raged, "Or the machinations of a hunter."

"What do you mean, a hunter?" Layla demanded. "Like that witch hunter thing you kept going on about? They aren't real. I mean, they were, but they never hunted real witches. It was just assholes who wanted to burn people they didn't like. Right?"

The demon's fires ceased spurting, but the shadowy wings rolling from his back didn't vanish. He darted his eyes to Layla and she gulped. "Right?"

"We are not safe here," Ink said. "And I think we know who they're hunting."

Slowly, he swiveled his head to Mikki, who'd shrunk into her seat. A blockade, hunters searching through cars to find a missing nymph. *The one that got away. Fuck.*

"What do we do?" I asked, my mind trying to churn with possibilities. What if I took Mikki into the fields? We could run for a time, try and catch a ride. Let Layla and the demon turn around for freedom.

Layla eyed Mikki. Or would she try to turn her in? An exchange of our freedom for the nymph? The stories of evil witches were legendary, dark fairy tales for kids, but whispers were growing between adults. People thought, with the rise in midnight raids and attacks, that it was the witches who'd turned on us.

"We get the fuck out of here," she said, her eyes meeting mine. "All of us."

Her hand slipped into her purse and the dangerous spell book appeared. "Here," she said, handing it to Mikki who'd been far too silent. With her chalk, Layla began to draw on the car's dashboard while Mikki limply held the book open. As she finished, a shimmer ran through the entire body of the car. I reached a finger out to follow the glittering spell, and my nail struck thick air. A shield covered the vehicle. Why?

Spinning back into place, Layla shifted the car into gear. "Everyone buckle up," she said, twisting the wheel. "We're going off road." The car shot forward, sending us racing over the dry fields. A cloud of dust erupted behind us leaving the hunters in the rearview mirror.

Chapter Fifteen

"Where the hell are we now?"

Switching from my phone to Layla's, I tried to get a signal. Country miles rolled past, gravel pinging into the car's chassis from the unpaved roads we'd found ourselves trapped on. It proved surprisingly easy to escape out into the fields, leaving the highway behind. Layla had spotted a farmer's wheel ruts, which led to a driveway and finally a service road. Since then, it'd been going downhill.

"It says…" I twisted her phone around, half a bar twitching up and reloading the GPS map.

Suddenly, the screen snapped to black and the low battery warning took over. "Fuck, it's out of juice," I said, glaring at the demon who'd been pouting about handing the phone over.

"So," he said, lifting the pink case from my fingers and shoving in the charging cable. "Crisis solved."

Except it'd take time to charge, and we'd been heading due west for far too long. The sun was already dangling in the sky. Even going under the speed limit, that much time through the fields could put us anywhere. An email popped up on my phone.

Yes! It got the signal from the waning cell tower. Raising it to my face, I was about to open the map when it dropped all service. *Damn it.*

"Cal." Layla's voice trembled. She'd been driving nonstop, her shoulders hunching deeper with every county mile we passed. "There's a four-way cross ahead. Do I take the road going south?"

I needed a signal. Leaning hard on the button, I rolled down the window. "Goddamn child…" I cursed at the six-inch gap it gave me. That had to be enough. Straining, I reached my hand through the window and wafted my phone in the air.

All it needed was to catch a stray electron, load the map and I could take a guess where we'd connect to a highway. With my cheek pressed to the glass, I stared up, watching the loading ball roll and roll and… *Yes!*

Lines, road names, even landmarks appeared. I began to tug the phone down when the car buckled. Half my body smashed into the door from the back wheel falling into a pit. It sent the car pitching to the right, which tossed Ink into me. His shoulder crushed my sternum, pressing all the air from my lungs.

Fuck, that burned.

I was about to reach over and shove him away, when my fingers clenched tight to the phone dangling outside. Whew, I didn't lose it. At that second, a large piece of gravel spun through the front wheel and shot clear through my phone.

"No, no, no!" I cried, prodding at the black screen as if the phone would work with a dime-sized hole in it.

"What is it? Do I go left?"

"I don't know. My phone's..." I raised it, causing everyone in the car to groan. Layla beamed sympathy eyes on me. I wanted to ruminate in her compassion, but the demon plucked the shattered remains from my hand and twisted it around.

"In my day, a good scrying crystal could withstand a rock or two," he said like he wasn't as deep into this as the rest of us.

"What about your crystal thing, Mikki?" Layla asked.

Mikki had been silent for most of the escape, an unnerving state for her. She hoisted up her crystal. "Afraid not. It mostly does photos, some video. Can't call anyone on it either. But... Maybe I could sense a road from the ground."

"You can do that?" Layla asked.

"Rub two sand grains together and I can tell you what you had for breakfast," Mikki declared.

Silence fell while Layla pulled the car to the side of the road without tipping it into a ditch. This felt like an 'everyone hold hands and pray' moment, but we didn't have many options left. We couldn't keep driving around nowhere forever.

Mikki cracked open the door and placed her feet outside. She shook her head. "Nope, need more." Without pause, she walked deeper into the ditch and down to the fallow field. Sighing, Layla shut off her car and slipped free. I joined her, both of us trailing after the nymph.

With her eyes closed and hands outstretched, Mikki kept pacing back and forth over the dirt. I winced at the torn-up stalks and clods on the frosted ground, but Mikki gave no hint of pain. She dropped down and scooped the snowy dirt in her hands. Rubbing it between her palms, she rotated her head on her neck and turned to us.

"I don't have a fucking clue."

Exasperated, Layla slapped both hands to her head and tipped back to scream at the sun. "Are you...? Okay. Okay. We turn south. That's got to get us closer to a sign, or a town. Even a goddamn farmhouse."

I reached out to rub her shoulders, but Layla dodged me and stomped back to the car. Mikki darted her gaze from the angry woman back to me. I couldn't say anything beyond my own shrug of exhaustion. And to think, I still had a fight with a werewolf pack ahead of me. Traveling was supposed to be the easy part.

"Get your ass in," Layla snarled at Ink, who leaned against the car door.

"As you say," he said with a deep bow, and slipped in.

She barely acknowledged him while shoving her keys in and turning on the car. The engine roared to life...until I opened my door and the steaming hood fell silent. Numb, we all turned to the front of the car and glared waiting for the hum of it to begin again. Like it was all a joke the car played on us.

"No. No, no, no." Layla cranked the key again, but nothing happened.

"Is it the battery?" I asked before noticing the dome light on. Probably not.

She slapped her hands on the steering wheel, her body bouncing in the sunken seat. "We're out of gas. Ha." That single, solitary laugh stabbed through my heart. I knew it well. The laugh from the edge, when there's a good chance I'm about to either scream or attack. Maybe even both.

Where the hell could we get gas? At least we still had her phone. But how could we call someone when we didn't even know where we were?

"What do we...?" I began, when Layla threw her door open, slammed both her feet to the ground and started to walk. "Where are you going?"

"I don't fucking know!" she shouted.

The demon and nymph hunkered into their seats, both refusing to meet anyone's gaze. Damn it. We needed to stay together. Wasn't that what people did? The second they split up the worst happened.

That's horror movies, dumbass. And in those, you'd be the monster.

"Stay here," I said, to Mikki. "I'll go get her."

The incubus snorted. "It'd be easier to geld the minotaur. But good luck."

I leapt out of the car, snatched Layla's coat from the trunk and raced after her storming silhouette in the distance. The sun streamed ahead of us, the last of its rays ready to vanish for the night of a full moon. Just what I didn't need.

* * * *

Nothing except the smoke of our breaths accompanied our hike across the godforsaken field. I didn't have to turn around to know the moon glared at our backs, its force tugging on the thread inside me. Layla marched a step ahead, her puffy coat an instant landmark for my weary eyes numb from the unending stretch of brown fields and blackening skies.

"How long do you plan to keep walking?" I shouted. My hands tingled from the cold seeping off the ground. It was nowhere near as bad as the winters back north, but it wasn't exactly traipsing-around weather. Especially not at night with no end ahead.

"Until we find someone who can help." Layla's words had the energy of popcorn bursting in the microwave. Random syllables struck my ears, trying to warn me about something. But even with my wolf hearing, I didn't get it. Maybe the damn demon could read her mind and tell me.

The demon...

"Why the hell didn't you ask your incubus to do this?"

Layla's march to eternity stopped. Her hair shook in the moonlight. "Are you fucking kidding me?"

Great. Maybe I wasn't even supposed to mention him.

"Why didn't I send Ink?" she screamed at herself, startling me.

The Jekyll inside me lifted its lips in a sneer. "That's what I'm wondering."

Bad move, wolf. Layla snapped around, the silver stream of moonlight landing on her face. "Well, why didn't you send your nymph?"

"Mikki can't fly. And she's not my nymph."

"Really?" Steam snorting from her nose, Layla stomped closer to me.

"Yes, really. Truly. I hadn't even seen Mikki for ten years."

"Until you saved her from a couple of armed attackers, then carried her in your naked arms."

Are you fucking serious? We're doing this now? What was I supposed to do? Leave Mikki to bleed out on the Kansas soil? Toss her a couple bucks for an Uber?

"What do you want me to say?" I asked, needing to break this stalemate.

Layla's lips pursed hard, her nose bunching at the top as if she was girding herself for a scream that'd rival a banshee. But when she opened her mouth, the anger evaporated. Screwing her eyes tight, she said, "That you want me."

An emotional kick shattered my ribs into my heart. I stumbled back off my high horse while aching to run to her side. Tell her that I did want her. Only her. That if not for her, I couldn't have survived this past month.

Bunching her hand tight, Layla snarled, "That you won't fucking run out on me."

Oh. So it's my fault, now. Leaping off my back legs, I landed in front of her. Surprise flared through her eyes but only for a second. I opened my mouth, expecting to feel fangs. The wolf was in charge without me even shifting. "What about you? How do I know you want me? That you desire me?"

"How do you…?" Layla grabbed the back of my neck and pulled me to her. A feral kiss struck through me, fast as lightning and caring nothing for the destruction it caused. She popped away, releasing her hold, and began to turn. "That answer your question?"

I clamped her forearm and yanked her to me. "No," I growled, knotting the back of her hair in my fist and kissing her. Layla twisted her fists into my shirt, tugging it and me closer to her body until the entire spread of her puffy pink jacket deflated against my chest. I pried her lips apart, needing more than a hard kiss of dominance. Lapping my tongue up the side of hers, I drank her scent. It embedded into my veins, carried by every red blood cell in my body. I knew her as I knew myself, and I needed more.

"Go ahead," the wolf jeered while yanking so hard on her jacket's zipper that it snapped off. I tugged her head to the side, letting me dig my nose into the hollow below her ear. With my teeth nipping against her throat, I dared her, "Think of your demon."

I bit. No cute nip, nothing playful. I wasn't holding anything back. Her skin tasted of a winter storm and the sweet drip of arousal. It drove my teeth in deeper, Layla squealing in my arms.

What the hell am I doing?

For a moment, the wolf faded, letting me stumble away from her neck that throbbed with a red mark. I checked to make certain it looked human, fearful of what fangs could do to her tender skin. *Shit.*

I tried to scamper away, when Layla dug her hand into my hips. Her eyes met mine, in all their wide, deepest pool glory. "My turn," she said and pulled my arm to her teeth.

The bite was nothing compared to what I had done to her, but the shock of it kicked through me like a shot of whiskey. *No.* It was the way her pupils dilated as she tasted me. The rise of her chest in a moan she could barely smother. The arousal beading in the air.

The ache knotted in my belly shot up through my chest constricting, screaming for a release. And Layla kept working her teeth up my forearm.

"Go ahead," I repeated my dare, dropping my open jacket to the ground and yanking my shirt off. Layla slicked her nails down my skin, goosebumps trailing her touch. My panting heat fought against the freezing night air.

I locked my fist to her shirt, ready to rip it in half. She grazed her bite against my chin and the urge to howl reverberated up my throat. I buried it in her mouth, my lips crushing hers while I tugged on her coat. Her sweet, soft arms. I caught a wrist, pulling her fingers to my pecs.

"Desire your demon," I said, cupping my hand to her breast. Flexing my fingers inward, I tugged past the cottony shirt and the bra. Her neckline strained, drawing my eyes to the rising curve of cleavage Layla tended to keep hidden.

Diving down, I bit right at the top of her breast. Layla cried into the cold air, "Oh, fuck!"

Her body trembled in my hands. I tossed her jacket to the ground on top of mine and toyed with her shirt, raising it so I could caress her breasts from under the band of her bra. *Get her naked, strip every trace of civilization from her bones and rut around in the dirt.*

Sense flicked into my head from deep in the throes of the animal. She would freeze. No. *Let Layla keep her shirt. Not as if you need her shirtless to ache for her.*

I grabbed my jeans, struggling to unbutton them as the fingers kept elongating to claws. The challenge made me more impatient, the wolf wanting to tug Layla to the ground then and there. I swung my head to the side, my ears trying to twist for the demon. Was he waiting to make an entrance?

"Let him watch," I growled, dropping my pants and grabbing Layla's hips. She curled her palm around my cock, jerking at the base and causing my leg to shake. All the hold I had evaporated, but I needed to concentrate to get her pants off. I bit her shoulder, Layla moaning in such delight that her pumping me paused.

"Who…who gives a shit about Ink?" she stuttered.

"You do." I stumbled. I had my palms wrapped around her ass and my fingers ready to plunge into her. "You pull him to you with your desire. You chose him over me, at home in the shower."

Frostbitten winds struck my backside. The heat of the moment began to slip from my fingers. Just like in the shower. The hotel. Why was I failing at this?

"Are you fucking crazy?" Layla said. Hooking her hand on my chin, she pulled me to her until our foreheads met. "I don't want him over you. I wanted both of you."

What?

"Right now," she said, gripping me so tight her fingers pressed into my cheeks. "I only want you."

I pushed my thumb inside her, her arousal demanding it thrust deeper inside. A groan slipped from my lips, the full rumble of it shaking the tender skin of her throat. She was wet, but not enough. Layla pushed her hips forward, grinding her clit on my hand. Her thrusts were determined and focused, her eyes gleaming as she held me under her spell.

Until I started to vibrate the whole hood of her clit against the tip of my claw. "Holy shit!" she shouted, careening her head to the side. Her legs began to tremble, more of her weight crashing on me. I tried to pull back, keeping the sharp edge of my claw from piercing the worst spot it could. Layla didn't make it easy. She clamped her nails onto my back, digging into the muscles flexed to hold both of us upright.

Her moans invigorated the wolf. It needed more. To have her scream in joy, to feel her quiver from the nape of her neck to her pinkie toe. To know she wanted this more than me.

My legs began to sink, Layla chasing after. She reached everywhere, tumbling against my hair, scratching an *S* down my chest, and finally circling around my cock. *Yes.* I fell to my knees, the cold ground radiating up the whole of my bare shins.

Layla.

Sense rose high enough for me to hold her, to push on her inner thighs and spread her above my narrow lap. To keep her from the freezing dirt that did nothing to slow the inferno inside me. "Cal," she whispered, her hips shivering so she kept brushing the soaked heat of her vulva against my cock.

Fuck.

"I want you. I want this—" Layla tugged on my cock, the head hardening until I wanted to thrust for her palm. "Inside me."

Are you certain?

It could hurt. I don't want to hurt you. I don't need to fill you.

I can, I need, I want...

Wrapping my hands around her ass, I pulled Layla flush above my cock. "Yes," I said, thrusting my hips up to meet her.

Her lips twisted into an *O* of shock and wonder. I caught her cheeks, holding that gasp from me entering her, that first perfect moment of mounting. Tugging Layla to me, I plunged my tongue into her mouth while rocking my pelvis. She slipped lower, the tightness of her clasping to me until I felt lightheaded. The taste of her was nothing but arousal, sweat and need, a sweet musk more potent than any perfume.

I reached around her ass, playing with the pucker, all the time watching to hear her cry out.

More. Deeper.

My leg popped up, the desire driving me to position myself. On one knee, I drove through Layla, sending her head careening back. The pressure of her cinching against me sent me reeling. I threw my head back, and a howl burst from the bottom of my lungs.

Teeth pinched around my Adam's apple. I stilled my head but kept thrusting, bouncing Layla on my cock while she pressed her bite deeper into my skin. Her arousal slicked down my palm, a deep groan rolling from her lips. *Go deeper, Layla. Harder. I can take it.*

Twisting my finger around, I extended the full reach of my claw, and flicked the whole of her engorged clit.

"Fuck!" Layla screamed, her voice shaking the ground below us. Her head flew back, the stars falling into her hair as she cried out from the orgasm racing through her. I watched, my hips stilled to keep myself from bursting.

How her eyelids shivered back and forth as she slipped into the throes of pleasure. How her lips parted, revealing a sliver of the gap in her front teeth. How her hands clenched at nothing. How the whole of her body trembled upon mine, the one that brought her bliss.

I bit her shoulder, Layla squealing in shock. Palming her ass, I thrust Layla onto me as deep as I'd ever dared. The wolf was nearing the brink — it had what it wanted in its sights. Layla held on to my shoulders for dear life, my ache sending me rising higher and taking her with me.

The end grew closer. Heat ripped through my spine and pooled from my inner thighs down. I felt myself slipping further into the feral control of the beast inside me.

Layla trailed down, pressing her palm right over my heart, and I came. There was no howl of ecstatic completion. Instead, I coated kisses to her sweet skin. Every touch cast warmth through my chest while my cock sputtered into her. This was a hell of a lot more than just a mating. She was a hell of a lot more than just a mate.

"Oh, fuck," I stuttered, falling back on my ass.

Layla managed to get her legs under her and rose off me. Before she went, I slipped my hand against her inner thigh, smearing the elixir of our session on my fingers. She was of a sounder mind than me, already tugging her pants up while I sat numb on the ground.

It felt like a whole month's worth of tension had erupted from that one session. I brushed the bottom of my aching balls, still sputtering out the last into the chilly air. The wolf was happy, but I had a few questions.

"Here," Layla said, picking up the clothes I'd scattered to the dirt.

I reached for my shirt, about to slip it on, when my always-held tongue finally got its turn. "Both of us?"

"What?" She swung back, her eyes widening.

"You said you wanted both of us. At the same time?"

Layla folded her head into her hands. I used the opportunity to stand and try to slip back on my jeans while nearly full cocked. "That's...it's Ink's fault. He put the idea in my head and, I mean, I'll talk to him. Tell him to keep the fuck away when we're uh, you know. No matter what."

"No." Only the sound of my fly zipping shut echoed from the fields. Layla froze so fully she didn't even breathe. "I don't...I don't like you doing that. Always pushing him away. Hiding him, as if what we're doing, what all three of us are doing is wrong."

"I just thought, I mean, that you wouldn't want to have to deal with him. With the reminder that there's an incubus around."

"But there is." I shook my head from the past month of minor annoyances finally crystallizing into an answer. "It's awkward as hell, okay, for you to keep arguing with him because of me. I don't want to pretend that we're normal. For fuck's sake, Layla, we're anything but normal. And that's okay. That's..." *A threesome?* I hadn't entertained the thought because she'd seemed so determined to keep Ink away.

Hmm...

Cupping my hand to her cheek, I pulled her shivering body into my arms. As she folded into my embrace, I raised her coat behind her shoulders. "I want you. To be with you. All of it, even the naked incubus parts."

"Really?" she partially squeaked, sounding beyond shocked. The occasional pique of jealousy would be a far easier issue to deal with than the constant tension of never knowing when another row would break out.

I pressed my lips to her forehead, wishing I could hear her thoughts from that touch. "Yes. We're all in this together. And I..." I couldn't live without her.

She looked up, her eyes glimmering with anticipation, and I completely chickened out. "Is that a house in the distance?" I said, pointing to the halo of light finally visible thanks to the sun setting.

Layla turned and took it in. "I think it is. We can get help and get the fuck out of here."

Holding her hand, we both headed off in the direction of the farmhouse. I leaned down to whisper in her ear, "You, me and Ink at the same time? Sounds fun."

Chapter Sixteen

The truck bed bounced, sending Layla tumbling into my arms. Her bright smile brought the same to my lips even with a tire iron jabbing into my spine. We'd found not only a house but the farmer, who'd been more than happy to drive us out to our car and fill it back up, though all he had was an old truck with his trusty hound sitting in the front seat to take us there. It was a real challenge to have to sit under the stars holding Layla in my arms as the indigo fields wafted away.

"Guessing that's it." Our new friend pointed to Layla's car sitting by the side of the undisturbed road. "How'd you say you wound up out here?" he asked, pulling up beside it.

I slid across the frozen bed, trying to move as fast as possible. The tailgate was gone, letting me drop to the ground and offer a hand to Layla. She took it with a twinkle in her eye that hadn't dimmed since our little detour in the field. Shit, I was probably grinning like a lunatic from it. *All those knots I wound myself into for nothing.*

Things were finally looking up. The farmer would fuel us up, we'd get back on a real highway, find a proper gas station then it was on to Santa Fe. And I didn't have to grit my teeth for the next slice of innuendo from the incubus.

Holding Layla's hand, we both walked to the car smeared in the unnerving glow of the truck's headlights. The back door swung open, and Ink rose to his full height. Before he could say anything, Mikki sprang from the front seat. "What in the ever-fucking hell took you so long?"

The demon chuckled. "We're lucky he wasn't employing his usual tactics, nymph, or we might have not seen either of them until dawn."

A blush caught in my gut, but I shook it off and walked past Ink. "Do you have anything to say about that?"

He laughed. "Are you accepting notes on your performance or should I utilize a one to ten scale?"

"Ink…" Layla warned, but I cut her off.

"Go ahead. Give me your worst."

His eyes lit hotter, the flames rising in the otherworldly irises. They danced to Layla and a smile rose on the incubus. "I'd say you performed quite amicably given the surroundings. While risking the threat of hypothermia can add to the suspense of a session, I would also advise avoiding it. All in all, an eight."

"Don't listen to him. It was an eleven," Layla said, but I didn't care.

The farmer shuffled out of his truck and carried over the plastic gas can. I dashed to his side and offered to take it instead. He shrugged, happy to let me cross the distance and tip what he gave us into the empty tank.

"So, you kids out for school?" the farmer asked, staring at Ink, then Layla.

"Yes, but the lesson is composed of your deepest nightmares and darkest dreams."

Layla grabbed Ink's hands and turned him away. "Nurses. We're nurses. We're in nursing school."

"Uh-huh." He watched her try to cram the demon back in the car. "Didn't think there was much call for nurses out here."

I heard the glug sound of the last of the gasoline slipping down the pipe. "See if that did it," I said to Layla. She abandoned her herding of Ink to turn the ignition. The engine caught without a single pause. Yes.

"Fin-a-fucking-ly," Mikki shouted, gliding across the hood of the car to land beside the rest of us.

The farmer stood up straighter, glaring at the woman who used a curse word in every sentence. Great. We did not need a fire and brimstone lecture. Ink would probably try to outdo him anyway.

"Thank you," I said, tugging out my wallet. "Here, let me compensate you for your trouble."

While I fished for a fifty, he jabbed a finger at Mikki in her midriff shirt, thin pants and no shoes despite the temperature ten degrees below freezing. "She...she's in there, too?"

"Mm-hmm," I said, passing him the money and the empty gas can. The farmer took both, but his eyes wouldn't break from Mikki who was growing more aware of it.

She twisted to him so fast her body blurred. Damn it, Mikki. Low profile. "You got a fucking problem or can we get the shit out of here?"

The kindly old man who'd skipped out on supper to fuel us up turned beet red. He looked at the stars and mumbled what sounded like an apology.

"I wasn't talking to you," Mikki said and jabbed a finger into my arm.

"Yes. Fine. We can go," I responded.

She squealed at the promise and dashed around the car to take the front seat once again. That left me sitting in the back with Ink, which didn't sound like quite the same punishment as before.

The farmer stared in awe at where Mikki sat. "That girl's quite speedy."

"She, uh, she did track," I said, hoping that excuse would be enough. "Thank you again for your help."

"It's, it's no problem. You all keep going down that road till you hit a stop sign, then go right. Follow the signs to a gas station."

I reached out to catch his hand to shake it, but the farmer kept it pinned to the gas can. Absently, I trailed my fingers through the cold air until they snagged in my hair. "Then we should get going. Thank you a second time," I said, bowing my head and keeping the man in my sights. Slipping into the right side of the backseat, I kept one eye on Layla who buckled herself into the driver's seat.

She released her grip on the wheel to trail her fingers back to me. Catching them, I brushed the tips of mine against her palm. The sound of the truck shifting into drive cascaded behind me. I was about to turn around, when the old farmer and his trusty truck rolled past and picked up speed.

"Ink, come on," Layla called. "Let's get going."

"Very well," he said as if we had startled him awake. The incubus folded his legs neatly to the side in the cramped quarters and buckled his seatbelt. "I do have a question, however."

Here it comes. I braced myself for any dirty, highly personal thought to flit through an incubus' brain. Ink kept staring ahead, trailing the twin red lights of our savior. "If the farmer's place of residence was behind us, where is he going?"

That... A niggling chewed on the back of my ear, but I shook it off. "He probably knows a good place to turn around."

"All I care about is getting on the road and finding somewhere to sleep," Layla answered.

"After your exertions, I am unsurprised. Do you require any ice for the strain in your loins?"

"Ink..."

They fell to a back and forth I was coming to know as friendly bickering instead of a cold war. Most of it passed me by as I kept staring down the dark stripes of the road. The farmer's lights were speeding up and about to vanish in the distance. Where was he heading this late on a cold January night?

* * * *

No one else lingered at the tiny gas station by the side of the road. It was so old that the sign didn't have any electricity. The numbers were hung by hand, and one of those garden spotlights lit it up. I didn't bother to get out of the car. Small towns weren't a safe place for a werewolf family that had escaped from a cult.

At least the gas tank was filled to the brim for our final push into Santa Fe. We all arrived at the decision to keep trucking forward. Staying another night anywhere could be dangerous, and besides, I needed to get to my mom. I'd offered to take over driving, but Layla insisted.

Too bad I couldn't call Mom to tell her we were on the way. I stopped pushing my pinkie through the hole in my phone and leaned back. A low rumble of music barely reaching past the front seats hummed under the girls talking. Something about Mikki's wing. Maybe Layla was checking on it. Or she wanted her own pair. Could…? A yawn strained my mouth apart. I tried to shake it away, only to send my gaze to the incubus.

He'd been staring straight ahead at what looked like nothing for a disquieting time. Or maybe demons slept with their eyes open. Who knew? The thought returned to me, wondering if witches could fly on brooms. Rather than bother Layla, I leaned for the seeming expert on the craft.

Hair rose clear down the back of my neck. My sense of hearing twisted, trying to home in on —

White. Blinding, deafening, white. Pressure slammed into the car and the world spun under us. I couldn't see but I felt the fear spiraling off Layla and Mikki. The force of their screams, no doubt overlaid with mine, weren't audible. But I knew them. My hands flailed out to catch anything, the force inside the car twisting it into a circle.

We kept spinning helplessly, my nose filling with the stench of gasoline and panic sweat. *No.* There was something else. *Lightning.*

"Layla…?" I called to her, my ears ringing through the cotton stuffed inside.

The scent of magic raced through the car. Was that Layla's doing? She must have been stopping our unexplainable spinning out. The G-forces ripping at my body slowed. A sheen of shadows began to form over my eyes, when the car slammed to a stop.

Fuck.

Pain thundered apart my skull. I strained to open my eyes, only for hot liquid to burn them. Red washed away the world, welling up my tears. It was blood. Blood from where?

Oh, my forehead. I winced, trying to stop the wound, when a blood-curdling scream erupted.

Mikki's seat thrashed back and forth. Wait, her door was open, light from the car streaming on a man in a suit. *Shit.* I fumbled for my seatbelt, only to find that the lock had been crushed in the crash. It wouldn't release, trapping me in place. Despite Mikki flailing and kicking, her body slipped out of the car and into the ditch we teetered over.

"No…" I yanked on the seatbelt, straining to rip it free.

The scuffle continued, Mikki not going down. Dirt rose from the ground, forming a brick that socked into the suited man's gut. He doubled over, letting Mikki run away, her body illuminated by the headlights. Her wings extended out, the glitter brighter than stars against the dark night.

A net erupted around her body. *Again.*

Who the fuck were these guys?

The net one walked past the car from the left, his gun still up. He was too focused on the nymph writhing in his trap. The driver's door slammed into his back. Layla smashed her hand to the tumbling man's neck and sparks burst through the air. *Her witch lightning.* The equivalent of a Taser on high just cooked through him, sending the attacker to his knees.

Layla slipped to the ground, her leg bleeding. She barely paused in running over the man to reach Mikki. "Hang on. I'll get you out." Both girls struggled against the net. They needed something to cut it. Something like me.

I didn't have a choice. Flinging my hand open, I extended the claws and swiped at the seatbelt. They cut into the polyester, peeling away the outer layer, but half the black strap inside remained.

Those men could recover. I slashed once more, when my bruised ears picked up a new sound. A van was approaching...and slowing. Every instinct in my body told me this wasn't a helpful Samaritan.

With one last scratch, wrenching my shoulder, I finally sliced the seat belt in half and jumped to my feet in the car. Where was Ink? I turned to where the demon had been, only to find an empty space. Great. Just when we needed him.

Forget that. Focus. Leaping out of the car, I watched the first man Mikki had bricked stumbling up. I folded my fist and slammed it into the back of his head. He cried in pain, but didn't crumple like I'd hoped.

Forget him. Get to the girls, then...

The van's door opened and a gun took aim directly at Layla. *No!* I launched forward, as if I could reach it in time. The gunshot rocked the van on its axle, smoke gushing in the cold air. It obscured everything, leaving me and the men in suits holding our breaths.

So fucking help me, if they hurt her, they weren't surviving this night.

"Ha." The woman in the suit who'd fired the gun laughed. As she did, the cloud of smoke evaporated enough to reveal Layla with her hand outstretched and a net caught around her invisible shield. "Looks like he was right."

Layla yanked her hand down, sending the second net tumbling to the ground. "I will destroy you," she said, holding both hands up. I wasn't certain what spell that was, or if she was bluffing. Either way, I needed to get her out of there.

"Nice try," the lone woman said. "Witch." Instead of a gunshot, or teargas, she threw out a piece of weighted paper. It flew with purpose, no winds catching it. Like a falling snowflake, it landed on Layla's shoulder and she crumpled straight to the ground.

No!

A hand clamped to my shoulder, spinning me around. I grabbed the arm and ripped. The crack of his humerus separating from the ball socket ripped through the air. The woman and her other lackeys in the van were eyeing me up.

Snarling, I spun, my body rippling with the shift.

Ah!

Pain seared up my leg. In shock, like I was watching from outside my body, I found a silver arrow shot clean through my lower leg. Mikki screamed every curse she knew into the ear of the man lifting her. And Layla...she wasn't moving. *What did they do to her?*

Gritting my teeth, I took a step forward. Agony sundered through my leg. The arrow was on a thick wire cable, my every movement slicing the metal wire deeper into my muscle and skin. *It doesn't matter. I need to save Layla and Mikki.*

They tossed their nymph prisoner into the van, and the man asked, "What about the witch?"

The woman watched over Layla. Was she even breathing? Was her heart beating? "Take her too."

"No!" I snarled, my voice warping into a howl. Adrenaline pumped through me, my body ignoring the unending pain ratcheting up my leg. I ran for them, my arms extending so my claws would cut both to ribbons. The woman stood before me, her eyebrow perched in amusement.

That's the first thing I'll rip off her.

Suddenly, my body slammed back. My chin struck the dirt, bouncing hard. White dots danced over my vision, blocking my view so the world faded in and out. Layla lifted off the ground. Her hand dangled until the tips brushed my hair. Van doors slammed shut, boots clomping through the gravel. One stood beside the driver's side door and the other...

I pushed up on my hands, knowing someone was beside me. A fist slammed into the back of my skull, blackening every sense I had.

Chapter Seventeen

"Wake up."

A hand flew through the air and I caught it millimeters from slapping my face. My eyes snapped open, only for pain to slam into the back of my head. What the...?

Ink's face loomed over me and it all came back. I moved to flip onto my stomach and stand, only for pain to seize up my leg. "Gah!" I screamed, running my hands down my tattered jeans to find those fuckers had impaled me to the ground. The wire cable ran back out of my reach.

"Where is she?"

"Where do you think?" I snarled. Clamping my teeth tight, I swung at the wire cable with my claws. "Sonnofa!" The cable bounced the arrow inside my calf, blinding me from the pain ripping through my entire lower half. Worst of all, I didn't even make a dent. Those bastards knew what they were doing.

Ink watched from on high, his arms crossed, while I crawled in the dirt, struggling to breathe. "Here," he said, and in one fell swipe, severed the cable clean.

Holy shit. I'd heard things about demons, but no one said they were that sharp.

Unleashed from the tether, I fumbled in the dirt, my brain demanding I run to the car. But my twisting only knocked the arrow around. I had to get it out before I could do anything. Except my mind didn't care about survival, about standing up, about anything except Layla. "They took her. They took her and Mikki, and where the fuck were you? Why didn't you save her? You let them take her and she could be..."

Shit. The sob of grief twisted into rage. Even crumpled at his feet, I snatched Ink's shirt and dragged him to my level. "You abandoned her."

Ink's eyes flared hot blue flames in the dark night. "Watch your words, dog. I was banished from the car when their concussion hit. Forced to watch from afar as they systematically attacked while you, foolish wolf, sliced your fingernails at them and Layla was taken."

Damn it. They were organized. They knew how to take down a nymph, neutralize a witch, a werewolf and a demon.

"Are you going to rise from the dirt to help me save her?" Ink demanded, his head crooked to the side.

"I am..." I raised my leg, only for the pain to shatter through me and send me tipping to the dirt. It wasn't Layla's hands that caught me but the unnatural chill of the demon. "I'm fucking trying," I snarled, my patience drained. Under my anger flared a panicking terror that I could lose her, and it was all my fault.

"Here," Ink repeated, this time wrapping his hand around my wound and squeezing.

Lightning hissed through my leg, every millisecond of his touch stabbing more pain into me. I felt myself about to vomit, to pass out, for my heart to implode. Then it stopped.

And the pain was gone.

The arrow's head was severed at the shaft, and the rest lay coiled on the ground. I tested my foot under me, finding I could put some pressure on it, but too much knotted around the cauterized flesh.

"My touch is not as healing as Layla's."

"No shit," I said, finally standing to face the empty road. Save the net left behind, it didn't look like anyone had been here. Tire marks drove into the ditch, their van turned around. "It'll do," I said, limping around to the driver's side. "Get in the car. Can you tell where Layla is?"

"Yes, but I'm not capable of drawing close," Ink answered, slipping into the passenger seat. He didn't fiddle with her phone, or stare nonchalantly out of the window. His wire-slicing nails dug into his pants, his eyes burning hotter with each second. This was the most focused I'd ever seen the demon, and it terrified me.

At least it could be used for good.

"I can," I said. Cranking the ignition, an old prayer to the moon slipped from my lips when the car started. *They didn't take the keys. They didn't sabotage the engine. They didn't think I'd get back up.*

Ramming the gear into drive, I slammed on the accelerator, hitting sixty, then seventy fast on the narrow strip of country highway. "You are aware what they are?" Ink asked, the loaded question hanging in the air.

Nets. Guns. Incantations. Wards. They had to be hunters, but I'd always heard they were a myth.

The demon's fires drifted to me, his skin crackling to black. As if sensing my trepidation at the idea of going up against what I'd always thought of as bogeyman, he asked, "Do you know what their kind are capable of?"

I drove my injured leg deeper to the floorboard, accelerating the car to ninety. The dashboard started to shake, but I ignored it. "You think I won't do everything I can to save Layla?"

Ink snorted. "Are you willing to maim, wolf? To disembowel, to shred, to kill?"

The sight of her plummeting like a puppet after the child was bored with it slammed through my mind. Clenching my teeth, I said, "Yes."

"Then we're in perfect agreement."

Every dark urge I'd tried to bury, to purge from my soul, played across my eyes. The taste of blood welled on my tongue and, for once, I didn't spit it out. *If they hurt Layla, if they escape with her...*

"There," Ink announced, pointing ahead of the dark road.

I couldn't see anything, the headlights off in the hopes of disguising our attack. But the demon was twisting in his seat, his wings trailing back and evaporating into black dust. Something was ahead of us.

"They are increasing speed," he said.

So were we. Pushing the pedal to the floor increased the car's speed until the vehicle started to shake as if it were about to burst apart from the velocity. How mad would Layla be if I killed her car? *Worry about that after she's safe.*

The full moon dipping to the horizon silhouetted the van. I kept speeding up, my eyes trained on the silver glint of the door handle on the back. All I had to do was crack that open, get Layla and Mikki and murder everyone inside. It became my point of obsession, the canine brain fixated to get it.

"Damn it," Ink cried, whipping my gaze away. His body slammed back through the seat without damaging it. I tapped the brakes, letting him catch up. "That's as close as I can get," he said. "The fucking ward is too strong. You, wolf. You need to destroy it."

"And how the fuck am I supposed to do that?" The overwhelming urge to ram into the van and send it toppling faded. Even if Layla's car could withstand that, the girls were inside and at risk from a rollover. "We could follow it, then free them from wherever they're being kept."

Ink shook his head, the fire in his eyes sparking outside in flammable lines. "No. Hunters will do the unspeakable in their lair. We must stop them, now."

Fuck. I unbuckled my seatbelt and rolled down the window. Sharp winds splattered against my shoulder, but I ignored them and hooked my hands outside. "Take the wheel," I said, already tugging myself out.

Ink leaned over and grabbed the wheel. He twisted it back and forth the way a child would mime driving and sent the car weaving. My stomach leaped into my throat, and I impaled my claws into the car's roof. At this speed, I'd be wolf tartare if I fell.

"What are you doing?" I snarled, embedding my ass into the windowsill as the car finally came under control. "Don't you know how to drive?"

"I am a two-thousand-year-old demon," Ink thundered, his foot pressing on the accelerator to ramp us back from the dropping speed. "Of course I don't."

Fuck. I started to slip back in, my plan already falling apart, when Ink waved me on. "But I am capable of learning. Go. Do whatever you must."

This is so stupid. So very goddamn stupid.

I kept repeating that in my head, the loop oddly comforting as I pulled myself out of the driver's-side window and slithered onto the roof. The world whipped past at eighty, maybe ninety miles an hour. Every inch was thanks to my claws plunging into the car's body. I flexed my muscles, fighting against the pull of momentum that wanted to slam me into the windshield.

"Get us closer!" I said, eyeing up the distance I had no chance of making. Only the bumper of the van was visible under the moonlight.

Whether the demon heard me over the roar of wind, I couldn't say, but the distance lessened. Crawling on my belly, I worked my way to the front. The roaring heat of the engine blistered across the hood, burning my front while my back froze. It set off a tornado inside me, my insides churning in fear and rage. The van grew closer and closer.

I needed to catch it. Impale my claws into its body and hang on. Just a little bit more. My wolf feet fully shifted, ripping apart my sneakers. Tattered bits of leather and nylon trailed through the air like confetti. That was why I only wore cheap shoes. Slamming one clawed foot to the metal, I started to rise, my knees bent.

The van filled my vision, its handle daring me to reach out and grab it. Just a little bit closer. One more inch. I lashed my hand out, my upper half tumbling, when the car slipped backward.

Fuck!

Every one of my abs tightened. With nothing to catch, my head crashed down. I tried to tug back, but there was nothing I could do against gravity. My chest slammed into the hood and I came face to face with the car's grill. Only the roar of the machinery churning us to our death filled my ears.

Rage fueled me to impale my hind claws, to slowly drag my ass back, and glare at the demon in the driver's seat. "What are you doing?" I shouted.

He clung to the steering wheel and stared at me. "I can't get any closer."

Even at this distance, I watched his hair tug back as if an invisible wall caught him. Damn it. I had to get to Layla, but I couldn't make it now.

"How close can you get us?" I screamed, my throat aching at the force.

The car revved and Ink shouted, "We're going to find out." I straddled closer to the hood, my knees bent. With one eye on the van, I watched Ink. His body flickered, like an old TV signal failing to come in. Slowly, his arms started to stretch, the elbows disappearing into the seat's upholstery along with his face. But he kept holding onto the steering wheel.

I focused on the van. Two feet away. An easy jump on the ground without the G-forces of a hundred-miles-per-hour pulling me back. I pushed my pads down, my legs hardening even with the arrow wound weeping down my fur.

"Wolf!" the demon shouted.

I leaped.

No second chance. Nothing to catch me. I jumped into the dark, unassailable air. My claws punctured the van above the window, my wolf body collapsing against it. I heard a crack shatter from the glass.

Shit. They had to have heard me.

Shit. They have guns.

Scrabbling, I hooked my back leg on the handle and clawed my way to the roof. In doing so, I rammed the handle open. The door swung free, casting the same turbulent winds inside.

"Close that door, Adam," the woman shouted.

I cricked my ears, trying to home in past the rush of wind and the screaming orders. A gun was cocked, closer to the right side than left. Beside the window. And a voice angry and faint. Mikki?

A gunshot burst through the roof from the back of the van. It blanketed away my hearing, leaving me to guess where anyone was. I dashed to the edge, one half of my body dangling from the side. The mad gunwoman kept firing up, clearly hoping to hear a yelp.

"For fuck's sake. Do I have to do it?" she screamed.

"No," Adam must have announced, his hand reaching out of the van for the door.

I had one shot at this. Crawling fully off the side of the roof, I stared down at the pavement whipping past. My stomach twisted, but I shook off the vertigo. Adam was straining. Maybe he had help. I kept hanging over the side of the van, pressing my feet against the window. It couldn't take the full weight of a wolf.

The glass popped. Was that loud enough to draw their attention? No time. The back door slammed shut and I reacted.

Feet first, I kicked in the window, my body flying upside down inside the van. While in the air, I twisted around, landing on all fours. A gun!

I bit her forearm, shaking it with the force of a shark. The woman screamed, her weapon tumbling to the padded floor. All the seats were gone, leaving me fighting in an open but confined space.

"Eve!" the Adam man screamed. He didn't have a firearm but picked up a long piece of iron left beside the window. I released the woman and stumbled back. She collapsed to the ground, blood gushing from her black suit. But the rage in her eyes told me she'd go for the gun again.

I kept backing up, my body pinned inside the cramped quarters of the van. At this angle, I gnashed my teeth at them and gave a swipe of my paw, but it was impossible to trap either of them.

"Hello, Big Bad Wolf," Eve said, stealing the iron bar from Adam. "We're under orders to take a werewolf in alive, but I can get you close enough to death for it to count."

Even with blood gushing down her arm, she swung at me. The iron clanged to the ground, an inch from striking me in the ribs. I collapsed against a warm body, my fur suckering around whoever it was. I wanted to turn, to see if it was Layla or Mikki. But I kept my eyes on the mad woman who only needed one more swing to crush my bones.

The demon. Where was that fucking ward? Eve swung and I jumped. Not at her, not to try and maul her face, but for a red symbol painted on the roof of the van. My claws struck, nicking a gap through the circle.

I landed right at her feet and stared, waiting for the angry incubus to crush them both. But Eve started to chuckle. "Is that all you have?"

"No."

My heart leaped at the voice. Layla dug her hand into my back, and she rose to her feet from behind me. Words I didn't recognize burst from her lips. The two hunters panicked, both running forward, when Layla smashed her hand to the ground.

The truck slammed to an instant stop. I jammed my claws into the floor, but they caught on cheap padding. The full force swept over me, sending my body bouncing against Layla. Just as I was about to crush her, I froze in the air.

Her face was bruised and cheek swollen, but a smile rose on her lips as she held me safe in her bubble. "I like this Jedi spell," she said and released it.

I dropped to the ground and raced to her. What did they do to her? Was she okay? Could we get her out of here? I nuzzled my head against her, hoping that would tell her everything my wolf mouth couldn't. She drew her fingers over my head and pulled me to her tearing eyes. It was bad.

"We have to get out of here," she said.

Mikki? I could only see the two hunters splayed on the floor. They were either knocked out or pretending. All it'd take was one shove of my paw to crack their spines. Leave them helpless and tossed to the ground like a used napkin. Just as they'd done to Layla. But where was Mikki? I couldn't abandon her either.

Layla spat on one and yanked a key off the other's belt. With it, she unlocked a chest bungee-corded on the side. Was this really the time to steal their shit? We had to find…

As she raised a jar out of the chest, my heart plummeted. Mikki was inside. Barely bigger than a doll, the nymph kept slamming her hands on the glass. Her curses carried up through the holes in the lid, though they were high-pitched and vengeful. *How do we get her back to normal?*

"Where's Ink?" Layla asked.

Oh god, the demon was still driving.

A massive squeal erupted from outside. I watched Layla flinch as she must have pieced it all together. The edge of the van rocked like something swiped the left bumper. With Mikki safe in her hands, Layla shoved open the back door. There was her car, with a good chunk of the front bumper smashed in. But it looked like it was still running.

The demon waved.

"Cal," Layla said, patting her leg to call me. I leapt to follow, giving one last kick to Eve's face as I went. "Here." She passed the jar to Ink and told him to get in the backseat. Taking the driver's side, Layla said, "Open it once we're on the road." She hopped into the passenger seat.

Sitting in place, I began to shift back. Layla adjusted her rearview mirror so we could both watch Ink pop open the jar. Mikki exploded from the glass, her face red with rage.

"I'm going to flay the flesh from every one of their bodies and give it to ghouls! Then bake their livers in a pie and feed it to wendigos."

Layla nodded and rammed on the accelerator. We blew past the van, Ink glitching out then appearing again as the hunters vanished in the distance. "I'll help you," she said. Her voice was nails in a blender, and I reached over with my human hand to touch her. Any part of her. To know she was here and safe.

I wound up bouncing her elbow, but instead of annoyance, she beamed gratitude on me. I could have lost her without even telling her. That had to be fixed. I reached for her, needing to kiss her.

"Did you not kill everyone in the vehicle?" Ink suddenly shouted, breaking us apart.

"No. Why?"
"Because the hunters are coming around for another go."

Chapter Eighteen

We blew through a sleepy old town, the solitary stoplight flickering at our indignation for refusing to obey. I didn't even have time to read the speed limit signs, the entire town blurring to a streak.

"They're taking the turn," Ink reported.

Layla had first tried outrunning them, which didn't work. Then she'd switched to taking random turns. *Also not helping.* On the plus side, they seemed to be out of those concussion grenades that had stopped us before. Now it was a simple matter of driving until one of us ran out of gas, and praying they went down first. Not really a good strategy, as the hunters were closing the distance.

The twisty streets of a town of three hundred opened up into the straight flats of a highway. *Shit.*

"Damn it," Layla cursed, trying to push her beleaguered car to reach beyond the ninety it danced with. "I don't understand. How did they shake off my spell?"

"Hunters are cheating fucksticks who think the only magic in the world belongs to them," Mikki snarled. She'd been shaking in the backseat, her wings straining and tucking back in to match her rage. At least she'd resumed her original height once out of the bottle. *I think.*

"I should have added two thousand pounds to their van. That'd have snapped the axle."

"No, you should have crushed them into a fine powder," Ink said. He'd been beating that drum for the past fifteen minutes. "Or allowed me to."

"For fuck's sake, will you let it go? None of us knew where the ward was. I was just lucky Cal managed to break the one pinning me down," Layla shouted at her blood-thirsty incubus and turned to me. But the truth was, I agreed with him. If I'd taken the time, found the ward and let Ink finish off the hunters we'd be in the clear. Instead, we were trapped in a fight I couldn't figure out how to win. They had the hardware, the counter spells, some tether arrow made out of industrial steel. If they stopped us again, we wouldn't survive.

"They're drawing closer," Ink said.

Layla yanked her hand off the wheel and rubbed it on her pants. Fear sweat beaded her forehead and I reached over to try and wipe it away before any dribbled into her eyes. She formed a terse smile as thanks, but the terror lingered. What had they done to her? What had they revealed they had planned to do?

"They're closing the gap," Ink continued, not helping.

"This isn't working. I have to get off this straightaway. They're too fast here." Layla started to crank the wheel, when Mikki grabbed her hand and pinned it in place.

"Wait," she said, her wings fluttering. Maybe it was the dark sky crammed over the endless horizon, but the golden sheen looked brighter than I remembered. "Don't turn."

"Are you crazy?" Layla asked even while keeping the car on the same path. "They're going to catch us. I see an exit ahead. If I..."

"Keep heading south!" Mikki shouted.

Layla looked at me, her lip tucked between her teeth as if she were trying to bite away the urge to scream. I started to rock on my naked haunches, the hair rising on my neck. It felt as if the hunters were breathing on us.

"I hate to throttle an expired equine," Ink said. Then his body flickered to sit between Layla and me. "They're on top of us," he announced.

The rearview mirror filled with the van's grill, its metal teeth gnashed in preparation for ripping us all to pieces. I reached over to hold Layla one last time before shifting. Ink remained in the way, so I hugged him too. One last fight for all three of us. My teeth sharpened and my ankles sprouted up. I turned my head, prepared to tuck my wolf legs under me to spring out and bite whoever opened the door.

A glow burned in my eyes. I winced, certain it was the hunter's headlights. But even with both sets of my lids closed, I could see it. *Feel the heat.* It swept across the entire car and out over the desert. Streaking like a line across the sands, the glow turned upward—a beacon into the night's sky. Mikki, her wings extended, flew up.

"I'm home," she shouted, phasing through the roof and into the stars.

"Mikki!" I called, certain the hunters had done something to pull her back. I tried to peer down through the back window, when Layla screamed.

A massive tidal wave ripped apart the ground ahead. It rose, the crest reaching five, ten, twenty miles above us. Layla shouted, "What do I do?" She couldn't turn the car away to outrun it, and we couldn't back up to avoid it. There was nothing to do but face it.

Our car pointed directly at the wave of sand extended so far above us that the entire sky was only the shadow of death. I tried to shift back, refusing to die in the fur, but there wasn't time. A whimper burst from my lungs, and I turned to Layla who looked at me.

I didn't even have a chance to tell her.

The wave struck.

No. It washed over us. Under us. It swept past, tumbling to innocent grains below the tires. In the rearview mirror, it reformed. Not into the wave, but a hand. A massive fist clenching around the van.

Squealing of tires unable to get a foothold burst through the dark night. It seared through my brain, itching against my gums, when the sound stopped. And the crunch of metal responded.

Layla slowed the car, but our momentum kept us gliding farther from the great fist of sand. I peered over the headrest, watching the fist warp. A bumper stuck out from the fingers, only to be crushed back in. Then a sharp metal edge. The sands trembled from their grip, looking like giant worms were rippling just under the skin of the fist.

It opened.

A dark mass tumbled to the sand, landing on a side until it tipped over. Dust burst into the air from its landing, obscuring whatever remained of the van burying itself in the ground from the impact.

"Turn around," I said, then reared in surprise I could. When did I shift?

Layla nodded, and did just as I asked, slowing the car to a near crawl. It wasn't the van I cared about or the people inside. The sands of the fist began to break apart into a fine glitter, each one shimmering like a golden waterfall until they formed the rising bodies of ten people. I watched them all form from the protective hand they'd created, some in dresses and robes like out of a futuristic RennFaire. Others were in jeans and hoodies. One had a Sheep Wars logo on it. But they all stood hand in hand watching us.

"Mikki," I called. She landed on her toes, then broke into a run. I cracked open the door, barely noticing if Layla had stopped the car or not. The ground rolled past my feet, but I was already running to thank our rescuer. "How in the hell did you...?" I started, Mikki laughing and pirouetting on the tip of her big toe.

"No one fucks with a nymph in her domain. You'd do well to remember that, demon," she said, jerking her head to Ink.

I reached back, taking Layla's hand in mine. Her other arm was around Ink's shoulder, both of us trying to support her. Ink tipped his head to Mikki. "Do you think I am foolish enough to try?"

"Manaliki." A woman who stood taller than everyone else, her white hair braided into a crown, called to Mikki. She strode forward, the blue trim on her tan robes glistening like a river running through the Gobi. Her black eyes stared through each of us.

"A demon."

Ink waved at that.

"A witch."

Layla quirked her lips to the side and shrugged.

"And…" the woman sighed, "the werewolf. Of course. Xek, loan him your robe so he need not freeze to death."

Ah shit. I clamped a hand over the bits of me I'd forgotten were on display. Near-death and saving the woman I loved had a way of blanking the naked problem from my brain. Xek drifted forward, his head twisted to the side and the robe extended. "Thank you, but I don't need…" I began. The nymph jabbed it at me and I took the robe. I was about to slip it on when I took in the slim physique of Xek and just knotted it around my waist, loincloth style instead.

The woman, whoever she was, snorted. "These are who you relied on?" She turned to Mikki, who shrugged.

"They saved my fucking ass, if that's what you mean, Zyna." Mikki snickered at the slow sigh from the woman in charge. Then she turned to me and a warm smile rose. "I'd be in a jar without them."

"You have our endless gratitude for returning Mikki to us," Zyna said with a slow bow. Then out of the side of her mouth she added, "Even the witch?"

"Yeah. She went all spell-fu to save me. Risked…I don't even want to know." Mikki reached over and took Layla's hand, the two softly shaking. Then Mikki tugged her closer and placed a soft kiss on her cheek. Layla opened her eyes in surprise, but as Mikki stepped back, Layla brushed her fingers over the mark.

"You know, if things don't work out with…" Mikki gestured first to me, then Ink. "Boy, you come with a lot of fuckin' baggage."

Layla laughed. "You don't know the half of it."

"I wish to reward you for all you've done. Not only for Mikki's sake…"

"Thanks, Grandma, great to know you care," Mikki interrupted.

Zyna barely paused in her declaration. She strode before the three of us and extended her palm. A small marble that glowed gold rested inside. "For saving nymph kind from all-out war, I wish to bestow upon you…" She started to pass the marble to Layla, but jerked back. "Upon you…" Zyna tried again, before turning and chucking it at Ink. "Just take this piece of the other realm."

"The other realm?" Layla asked. She picked the marble up out of Ink's hand and gave it a little shake. Zyna jerked at that, as if she was about to yank back her present.

"A witch that does not know of the other realm. Who rescues nymphs? What are you?"

"*Pst*," Mikki said, jerking her head to the side. I followed her away from the older nymph either schooling Layla or arguing with her. Probably both, judging from the sound. At least I knew Ink would protect her.

We paused in the cold indigo dunes, the full sphere of the moon lingering just before its final dip to the horizon. All my life I've hated that thing. What it does to me, the threat it poses. But if it hadn't been full tonight, I never could have survived that jump. I would have lost Layla, and that fact fermented in my stomach.

"I think I can take it from here, Cal," Mikki said. "Gram and her troupe will see me back to Arizona proper."

"Good." I nodded. At least something had come of this. We'd got Mikki home to her family. I still had to face what remained of mine, and the threat this game of alphas and packs put on it. Exhaustion I'd been fleeing from the whole night finally crawled over my brain and sunk in its fangs. But even with my shoulders sagging and legs about to give out, I watched Layla.

At least she was safe.

"You know, she's all right. For a witch."

My cheeks burned at having been caught, but I nodded. "I know."

"You know you love her too?"

How did she know that? Mikki smiled at me, my shocking response her answer. She'd been fishing in the dark and hit a bullseye. With a strained chuckle, I said, "I'm beginning to suspect that."

"So go tell her. You know, before some jack-holes with an RPG and helicopter drop in and fuck up your life."

I laughed with her, my fingers twisted together so I could hold them in place. Tell Layla, take every wrong in my life and put it in hers.

"What about you?" I asked, turning it on Mikki. "Are you okay? Really okay."

Mikki lifted a shoulder, her smile oddly wholesome for the nymph who cursed like a sailor who'd slammed his dick in the door. "I'm home. For the first time in god-fucking-ever, I'm home. Now it's your turn."

"Hm?" I asked, watching Layla shake her head in exasperation from Zyna's prodding.

Wrapping her hand around me, Mikki whispered in my ear, "It's time you got home too."

* * * *

As the car turned to the south, on the right path to hit Santa Fe in five hours, the desert nymphs gave us one last show. They folded together into a golden butterfly made of sand. It hovered in the indigo sky, waving goodbye one last time before turning to the west and Arizona.

"How's the leg?" Layla's languid voice curled down my ear. If we hadn't just spent the past night in mortal terror fighting for our lives, I'd have tossed her onto her back and kissed her. Instead, I wrapped my arm around her side and pulled her closer.

As she nestled her head on my shoulder, I said, "Much better. Thank you." Kissing her on the forehead, I rubbed my calf that was healing from not only the arrow wound but the demon flesh-searing of before. It was good to have a witch girlfriend.

"I can't believe..." Layla began, when her mouth stretched into a wide yawn. Shaking it off, she cupped her hand over my thigh and said to the front of the car, "Since when can you heal?"

The demon we let keep driving snickered. "I have numerous talents, my bond. You've only been privy to a small sampling." He twisted around the rearview mirror so both Layla and I could watch him wink.

"Uh-huh," she muttered, obviously not impressed.

We'd survived. The attack had been so fast, it was as if I'd mourned her loss and rejoiced at finding her in the same breath. Which left a lot of conflicting emotional dominoes yet to fall.

Layla's hair tickled my nose as she settled her head more comfortably on my chest. Even buckled in, she kept straining to reach me. Pulling closer and closer until she was almost in my lap. I didn't want to let her go.

Smoothing down her flyaway hair with my chin, I nestled my lips right on her crown. "What you did, charging for those hunters. Throwing yourself in the way to save Mikki..."

Ink grunted at that. It was obvious he didn't approve of Layla's heroics. Or maybe he thought it should have been me that wound up in the hunters' net. I didn't care.

"It was the right thing," Layla mumbled, brushing her cheek against my naked chest.

I held her tighter, the domino of fear tumbling in my heart. If it weren't for Mikki's grandmother, if I hadn't gotten lucky slicing apart that ward, I could have lost her. Hunters were notorious for using werewolves as sport, forcing us into form so they could hunt us for their amusement. But what they did to witches... My body shivered at the thought.

"Don't do that again," I said.

Layla didn't respond but Ink added, "Please."

I nodded in agreement, my words melting into a chittering pain as they fell out. "Being without you. Facing life without you. I...I can't." This woman I'd fantasized about for years, helplessly crushed on from afar, needed in order to cling to life was in my arms. And in all that time, I hadn't told her the truth. Tucking back her hair, I placed my lips to her ear and whispered, "Layla, I love you."

My entire body clenched from the biggest truth of my heart escaping into the world. What would she say? Would she laugh it off? Panic?

A soft sigh escaped from her lips, the warrior witch asleep in my arms. Chuckling at my terrible timing, I leaned back into the seat, holding Layla tight. I could always tell her in the morning.

Chapter Nineteen

Desert winds caught the red and white stripes, snapping the maple leaf flat against the red skyline. Filthy dirt rattled off the road, scrub brush and a tattered wind fence hiding the stucco walls. A smile began to tug my lips at the nearness of home, when I turned down the narrow drive that tipped nearly forty-five degrees, and my heart stopped.

SUVs and trucks lined the entire dirt road, making certain to pin in the old VW bug covered in dog stickers. I was too late.

Layla patted my knee, causing me to jerk forward in the driver's seat. I was trying to read the license plates crowding around. They ranged across the entire southwest, the vehicle paint showing faint scratches and dents. From wear and tear of the road or the people who'd challenged the pack?

On autopilot, I pulled into the sand pit I'd always parked in after school. My legs were already on the move, when I caught Layla unhooking her seatbelt.

"Stay here," I said, snagging her hand and pinning it in place.

"What the shit?" she responded.

"The pack is already inside." My heart thundered in my ears, blanketing any tell-tale sounds the wolf should hear. What if I was too late? What if they decided I wouldn't show and took their vengeance?

Layla twisted her head, taking in the swarm of backup. "Yeah, I figured. Which is why I should —"

"Stay here," I interrupted, once again locking the seatbelt back into place. Damn it, I didn't explain to her how dangerous a witch walking into a werewolf gathering was. With her glaring at me, the paltry explanations I'd thought of all faded to useless gawping.

Only one idea flitted through my mind. Holding the nape of her neck, I pulled Layla to me and whispered, "I don't know what's inside, and right now I need to know you're safe. Please."

An exasperated snort answered me, but she nodded her head and sat back.

"Ink?" I called to the demon.

He sat up from the backseat, his face beaming. "I shall keep our dear most delightfully entertained in your absence." Reaching to the front, he caught Layla's hand and pulled it to his lips.

That wasn't what I meant, but it'd do. Nodding, I moved to slip out, when Layla locked her fist around my shirt. "If anything happens, I'm storming the fucking castle." She pulled me to her for a hard kiss and let go.

I hurried away, my lips stinging not from the force but from a growing concern that it might be my last. My mom's windmill spun on the rising winter storm, the trio of Dutch girls on the base churning butter at breakneck speed. I stared at the site so familiar from my childhood that I'd stopped noticing it.

The front door wasn't locked. She never did. Hard to know when those wayward wolf sons would stroll in from a desert run, naked and hungry.

My mom didn't back down from a fight. She'd escaped an alpha on just wits alone. But against that many werewolves... The old ache started again, the taste of blood welling down my throat. I shook my head hard, willing myself to grip the handle and pull.

A cold blast struck my face, the A/C aimed right from a vent over the threshold. I shivered to my naked feet, my toes flexing on the old doormat of daisies and plastic grass. The woosh of air covered over any soft sounds, but the scents were wrong. I knew my mother's house, our house, by the twists of her incense in the sitting room, the cardamom in the kitchen, the combo of testosterone and dog in our bedrooms. Now, it was all tamped down by the stench of men and danger.

I took a step forward, trying to pad as quietly as possible. *If they have her at gunpoint, surprising them is very unwise.* "Mom!" I shouted like I was twelve and running home after a never-ending day of trying to hold still.

Easing past the line of frames stuffed to the brim with images of us from age ten and up, I stared into the sitting room. Five men sat nearly on top of each other on the old desert rose couch. They were so heavy that the plastic covering warped from their mass, the sides straining to the point of ripping. I didn't know any of the men dressed less like cult leaders or gang members. The predominant uniform seemed to be polos and dockers, though the three-quarter sleeves didn't hide the range of tattoos I knew to be pack signs.

I blinked, willing my eyes to see that there was no body left lying on the floor, no blood welling into the baseboards we'd once chewed off. "Mom?" slipped from my lips, when a flurry of turquoise jewelry knocked into itself.

Arms wrapped around me, pulling my forehead straight to the massive necklace she'd always worn. I sat stunned for a moment, my mind in shock that she was alive and capable of hugging me. Slowly, I locked my arms around her, trying to erase everything that happened with Mark, with the asshole. With Eli.

"Where the hell have you been?" she snarled in my ear.

A stupid laugh rattled in my throat. "It's complicated."

"Is this him?" the fifty-something man in a navy polo with gold embroidery on the pocket asked. He rose from the couch, leaving the rest of the men to try to look imposing while sitting on an old lady's sofa.

"Yes." My mom nodded. She moved to the side, but wouldn't release me. "Calvin, these are the members of the Justin pack."

"Justin?" I snorted, only to be answered by a low growl from all five and another behind. Glancing over my shoulder, I spotted two more men standing in the hall. They must have been waiting in the kitchen. How many were here?

My mom's gaze darted to the same thing, her face telling me to watch myself. Formality mattered more than the truth when it came to werewolves. And failing to show proper obedience was answered with a fang to the throat.

With the hair rising on the back of my neck, I focused on the leader. The alpha. Most likely Justin himself. "You requested my appearance?" I said. My hands dangled loosely at my sides. No threat…but also ready to transform in a second should the worst come to pass. I tensed my legs, regretting I only had a pair of track pants left after losing my jeans. They swished with every minor movement of my lower half, no doubt ready to give me away should I shift to attack.

Justin stepped closer, his face meatier than I expected to find in a wolf. They all looked as if they'd eaten an entire herd of deer, these wolves growing fat from the people under them. It wasn't an easy thing for a werewolf to pull off. Some of us died of emaciation if we weren't careful. It paid to be the biggest asshole in the rectum forest.

"Tell me, pup," Justin began. My mom grabbed my fist as if she expected me to clench it, but I wasn't stupid. Even the wolf prowling behind my eyes knew we wouldn't get more than two swings in before they buried us. "Is it true that Alpha Lucien is dead?"

Every eye burned on me. Lying to an alpha was a corporal offense, which was why we'd always been on the run. "Yes," I said, holding my heart steady.

Justin took in my answer, his nostrils flaring to try and sniff out the lie. It wasn't unheard of for one pack to draw out another by pretending an alpha had died. But he smiled, showing off a single silver fang between his teeth. "As it was so recorded in the annals."

"And on Twitter," one of the backup wolves added.

That drew Justin's glare, silencing the other man who couldn't be more than a few years younger. "What I want to know is why you'd first returned to the pack's hunting grounds. Did you not flee from the alpha's range?"

My mom dug her fingers into my skin, her heart pounding faster as she eyed up the wolf threatening her and her babies. It was my turn to try and keep her from attacking.

If Justin was aware of the women ready to rip his throat out, he gave no hint. He didn't even glance once at her. "Did vengeance drive you to return?"

"He went there for school!" my mom shouted, shoving herself into the alpha's face and forcing him to acknowledge her. "Like I said. He's going to med school."

There was pride, as always, but I heard the terror lurking in her voice. I'd heard it damn near every night when she'd have to talk to the asshole, have to pretend that she was happy and deserved whatever he did to her.

Justin eyed me up. "Is that true?" His tongue flicked the silver fang as if to remind me what he could do if I lied.

Yes. I was in college for nursing. I'd been there for years before everything went down. I...

I held my breath and met him eye to eye. "No."

"What?" my mom shrieked. "That's not, he didn't go there for revenge. I swear. Cal. What are you doing?"

Her words fell on silenced ears, Justin shoving her to the side. I tried to reach to catch her, but he clamped a hand to my throat. "Funny, your bitch tells a different story."

"She didn't know. None of us knew until the ass...until Lucien told us." I gasped, fighting my urge to struggle out of his grip and also pluck out his eyes.

My claws kept pushing free, demanding I shred him to pieces for touching me.

"Told you what?"

"He called us. All of us. Me, Mark…Eli. He brought us to him. I don't know why!" There was the truth, the whole of it. I didn't want to believe that I wasn't finally past those biologic confines of the monster who made me. But all he had to do was flip some switch and it sent us running to him.

Justin stared me down, his face millimeters from mine and the stench of vodka and vape juice on his lips. I could count the number of scraggly beard hairs poking from his chin. It wrenched my stomach, my heart frozen waiting for his answer.

"Ha," the alpha laughed once. Then a second time. Soon the others picked it up, short bursts of disgust erupting from their mouths. My spine shuddered at the noise and Justin released me. "That fucking idiot. He put in a Call to his young without any backup?"

"Calvin?" my mom whispered in my ear. "Did that really happen?"

Numbly, I nodded my head. Old prayers slipped from her as she tucked me closer. "What is the Call?" I asked her as quietly as possible, but no one can whisper around werewolves.

"Don't you know?" Justin spun on me. "Your bitch didn't teach you anything. The Call is a challenge, a test for the alpha to prove that he has earned his status. And whosoever unseats him, well…"

Becomes the new alpha. My body locked inside my mother's embrace. It wasn't supposed to happen, but Justin caught the flex of my arms and his laugh shifted to piercing suspicion. "Which one of you killed ol' Lucien? I'd love to give him a pat on the back."

He couldn't even bother pretending that last part was genuine. Greed rippled off Justin, the alpha eyeing up an opportunity to expand his territory. All he had to do was wipe out the solitary wolf and his mother in their quiet country home.

It wasn't me. I didn't do it. I didn't challenge him. Or see Eli's limp body in my mind with every slice of my claws through his flesh. Or feel Lucien's belt with every snap of my jaws. I didn't bite into his neck, my fangs didn't sever his arteries and rip out his trachea. I didn't do it.

"Mark," I said. My heart stopped, my breath stilled and my mind blanked to white. No. There was one thing in there. Layla, in her purple jacket with the black fur hood, smiling at me. It was all I had to cling to.

The stench of Justin's body, both wolf and man, washed over me. He leaned closer, his beady eye nearly in mine. If he thought I'd lied, if he'd heard differently, if he knew he'd get away with it, I'd be gone.

Saliva dripped down his silver fang, the alpha snickering. "Had to be the fucker who up and vanished. Oh, well. That's the Endless Moon's problem. Come on, guys. Let's get the fuck out of here."

And just like that, the massive pack who came to seek revenge on the death of another alpha trailed out of the house. Some even took the time to gather up the shoes they'd left at the door. I reached over to hug my mom, uncertain if I was holding her up or she me.

Justin waited on the side, directing his men with a single word or nod. Just before he left, he said, "Keep out of our territory, packless. Or you won't like what happens next."

I closed my eyes, the compressed tension uncoiling from my muscles. The front door began to swing closed, allowing me and my mother to hide away from the politics of packs and alphas. Suddenly, it flew open.

With hands wide, a book in one and the other holding a marker, Layla dashed inside. "Are you okay?" she shouted, her eyes wide.

I laughed in joy at her running to protect me. "Yeah," I said, my chin jerking quickly. For the first time in ages, I felt okay.

Chapter Twenty

"Please, eat up," my mom said, pointing to the massive plate of rice and beans she'd left for Layla. I could already read the strain on her face. The human digestive system was not designed to handle the amount of a food a werewolf mother could cook. But Layla lifted her fork and picked a small section off.

"What about you, young man? Er..." My mom paused, her teeth bared at the demon quietly sitting in the kitchen by the rows of succulents.

"I haven't been young in a thousand years," Ink said. "And I've never been a man, come to think of it."

"Right. Calvin, why don't we let them...?" She tipped her head at the door and I stood up, leaving my half-eaten plate behind. Even with the pack gone, I couldn't escape the nerves rattling in my stomach.

And I was glad my mother didn't harp on that, for once. She slipped into the sitting room while I lingered, watching Layla poke at her food. Ink reached over, took a massive forkful and crammed it all inside.

"Oh, thank god," Layla said, happily scraping all her food onto Ink's plate. She must have caught me staring as she paused and her cheeks burned.

Chuckling to myself, I found my mother looking at one of the triptychs on the back wall. We each had one. The first image was one of the very first pictures ever taken of us out of the cult, dirtied and uncertain of what freedom meant. The last was our graduation photo, hats tipped awkwardly to the side, tassels in our eyes. The middle was harder to explain to friends — a young dog sitting as straight as possible.

It was Eli's she stared at, tracing her scarred fingers down the middle of the white wolf pup. "I promised I'd protect him," she said softly.

Shit. The river of tears that I'd thought had finally run their course found new life. I punched my fist to the side of my head, trying to stop them before worse started.

"Trisha begged me to get Eli out the night before the bastard finally... Before she died."

I didn't know that. Did Eli?

My mom never talked about the compound. None of us did except in codes and whispers. Mark would twist curse words to act as euphemisms, and Eli... He'd pull me into the old horse trailer we'd found rotting in a ditch. Only there could he mention the cult or our father by name. It was the safe place. He couldn't get us there.

"I'm so sorry," I gasped, my heart bleeding that I'd never see my brother again.

"Oh, sweetie." She wiped at her eyes, scattering the mess of tears and her mascara. I fell into my mother's arms like I was five years old and trying to hide from the whip. "It's not your fault. None of it, nothing was your fault. It was his. Every torturous day. Every...night. He did it. And now he's gone."

She sounded as if she couldn't believe it. I barely did. The asshole had never really left us. A pack could report us to him. He could send members of the cult after us. And that face greeted me every morning in the mirror.

"He is gone? Right?" she whispered in a voice we'd all passed around those first months bruised and bleeding, struggling in our new freedom.

I nodded succinctly. "Dead certain," I said, flexing my jaw and getting an ache for it.

"Good. Good. I know it's terrible for me to say, but I'm glad it was Mark who did it."

"Mom?"

She released me, already wiping her eyes clean, a smile snapping over her face to hide away the depths of her grief. We all learned that one too. "I love him, I love all of you. But your brother, he...he couldn't be swayed from his revenge. He needed it to keep going, to guide him. I'm just happy that you aren't caught up in the pack politics."

Whoever kills the alpha becomes the alpha.

Iron drenching down my throat, eyes burning from the spray of blood splattered across them.

"Cal?" My mom tugged on my arm, shaking me from the memory. Her eyes were narrowed, watching. Did she smell the truth on me, or the other truth we all had to believe?

"I wish I knew where Mark was," I said, hoping that'd cover for me.

My mom sighed. "He'll probably appear when we least expect it. That was always his best trick." She smiled winsomely, perhaps thinking of the boy that once had managed to shift in a security office without being caught to sneak out via the ducts. "What about his mother?"

I shook my head. "She's…too far gone."

"I'd hoped he'd, that he'd at least find peace with her. She…"

There was no need for her to go on. I knew best of us all how Mark felt about his mother. *Traitor* would be the kindest word he'd ever used. It hadn't been his mother who'd asked mine to save him. Mark — at only seven years old — had had to do it himself. Because he'd known that if he stayed under Lucien's belt, he wouldn't live to see age ten.

So much evil that didn't come from hell's dominions, or the nether realm's monsters lingered in our past. It was the banal evil people turned a blind eye to every day. An unexplainable bruise, a quiet child, a downcast face. A fear to breathe wrong or face a broken nose. A tremble in bed that the creaking floorboards could be a father filled with wrath and needing a soft body to take it out on.

But we'd been more than that. Eli, he'd used to make puppets out of junk we'd find littering old farmhouses. Mark had been a kitten magnet, even in wolf form. We'd had a constant stream of cats giving birth on our porch. Every night, Mark had made certain they were warm and fed. No matter how hard the asshole had tried to divide us, to pit us against each other, to surrender to his hate, we'd been a fucking family. *That he couldn't take.*

"Am I allowed to ask about the witch?" my mom said, jerking me to attention.

"Layla is…"

"A magic user," she said, then tapped her nose. "I know. Calvin, are you certain—?"

"About her? Yes. She's not like…" I squeezed my eyes tight, realizing I didn't really know any other witches to compare her to. "She's important to me. She's—"

"You love her?" my mom asked as a question that came off more like an accusation. I didn't know how to answer, my shoulders rolling like a wave. "You know…" She glanced up at the door, before leaning closer. "You can't have children with her?"

"Yes, Mother. I know how that works. It's not something—" *I stopped to think about.* Being with Layla was the answer. I knew that in my heart. But I didn't consider what my life with her would fully mean. "I'm not worried about it."

"Really? You were obsessed with Eli when he was a baby. I used to sneak the two of you under the floorboards just so you could play with him," she said, her voice light. "I'm surprised his first word wasn't *Cal.*"

"Mom," I said, clenching my hands together. "Please."

"I'm sorry." She pulled me closer. I'd overshot her in height when I was sixteen, but my mother towered over me. To think, she'd been my age when she'd turned on the cult, taken three young boys into the woods and lived off whatever scraps we'd been able to find. She'd saved all of us. "Is she kind? Your witch?"

"Yes."

"Does she care for you? Protect you? Help you?"

"All of those and more. Layla would…" It wasn't that she'd die for me—she threw herself in danger for a near stranger. It was that I could lay my head in her lap and know I'd wake safe.

"Then—" my mom began, when she looked up. I followed to find Layla with her phone in hand. She caught both of us, winced and turned back around. "Be with her as long as you can." She released me and walked to the hall to wave in Layla.

"And, Calvin."

"Yeah?"

"Don't shift in your shoes. It leaves leather bits embedded in your toenails," my mother said, a last piece of advice. I stared down at my feet, noticing the specks of green and black I'd missed for the past day.

A warm hand caressed my shoulder and worked back to the nape of my neck. I smiled, slowly lifting my eyes while I held on to Layla. "Hey," she said, bumping her nose into mine. "How're you doing?"

"I was about to ask the same."

"Well…" She nipped her lip as if to keep in her thoughts, then said, "If I have to sit for another of your mom's meals, I'm afraid my stomach will explode."

A hearty laugh rolled through me. "Years of having to feed three teenage male werewolves. I don't think my mom knows how to cook anything less than a full thanksgiving dinner anymore."

"Is everything…okay? With the pack stuff?" Layla tacked on fast, but I could feel the lingering question. *What did my mom think of her?*

Drawing my thumb down her cheek, I caught her chin with my fingers. "For the first time in my life, it's good."

"Which part?" she asked.

I pulled her to me, the invigorating scent of her magic filling my veins. Her lashes fluttered over the deep brown eyes, the tiny flecks of green catching the southwest sunlight. "All of it," I said, kissing Layla.

"Oh, is it group time?" Ink shouted, running to throw his arms around both of us.

"Ink!" Layla began, but I laughed and kissed her again even with the demon's lips against her ear.

"In time," I said. "After I've gotten a good night's sleep. Week's sleep, probably."

A blush burned up Layla's cheeks, hopefully her desires running rampant with ideas. Ink slugged me on the arm and said, "I knew you liked me, wolfie."

* * * *

Not even the snow under my truck's tires had melted in the week we were gone, almost as if nothing had changed. I caught the flutter of Layla's hair from the heater's blast and smoothed it back. She turned from my touch, her smile rising, when the third member of this whatever group rose from the backseat. Instead of glancing away, or Layla telling him to sit back, she leaned over to kiss me, then twisted in her seat to catch the incubus' hungry lips.

I waited for the knot in my stomach, the clench in my jaw, but only an effervescent calm radiated around us. This seemed to be working.

"Got you home," Layla said, retracting her seatbelt but staying inside the car.

I nodded, also not reaching for the door. The cold, wet world of having to fix my truck, my phone and prepare for tomorrow waited. I wasn't in a rush to abandon the heat.

"If it's all the same," Ink said, tossing Layla's phone into her hands, "I'm returning to the couch."

"Why? Did you run my battery down?" She laughed, checking the screen.

Ink scoffed. "Hardly. There are an entire three percentage points remaining. Demons simply don't do goodbyes." With that he vanished, leaving me and Layla completely alone.

It'd been a relatively quiet return home, the demon doing most of the driving. My mother had asked me to stay, but classes started up in two days. I still had books to get and my schedule to figure out. I'd missed Santa Fe, that old stucco house on the edge of the city with horses for neighbors and an endless sky above. But sitting on the plastic couch, eating off the old green vine plates, I'd felt small. *Cramped.*

All my life, the answer had been running. The cult pressing in? Run. Schools questioning our forged documents? Run. Packs sniffing where they shouldn't? Run. I'd stood my ground here, where it all began, because I'd thought my father forced me to. Because his blood had twisted the wolf inside until I had no choice.

But that wasn't it. I wanted to be here, even with him gone, even with the whole world open to me. I wanted to be with her.

"You could come in," I said while Layla prodded at her dying phone. "Maybe for some hot cocoa?" *Oh my god, that's so stupid.* When I didn't hear her snicker, I said quickly, "Or, I might have some, uh…" My brain tried to scroll through the remaining liquor cabinet but it wasn't looking good. "Marshmallow vodka?"

When she didn't look up, I feared I must have said the wrong thing. But the longer it stretched on, Layla's forehead furrowing deeper, the burr of concern kicked around in my gut. "Layla?"

"I got a message from Mikki," she said rapidly. "Here."

Taking the phone, I tried to focus on the small text while saying, "She's already emailing you?"

Layla blushed hard. "Well, she knew your phone was busted and... Just read it."

Laughing, I focused on the mile-long text.

Good news, Claw. I made it home and without starting an inter-realm war. There will be no massive nymph slaughters on my head. My mom was furious about the hunters. No one knows where they came from or how they knew. Weird thing though, seems I wasn't let go from the river nymphs out of the kindness of their heart. Or a need to use my room for a new gym. Some outsider paid for my freedom. A Mr. White. Don't suppose you know him?

Her head flew up. "Mr. White? Again?"

I shrugged. "It could be a coincidence. Lots of Whites in this world."

My father had thought a Mr. White was going to invade his pack and that Eli was working for him, which had turned out to be an utter delusion on his part. Eli had wanted him dead, the same as the rest of us. He hadn't needed any outside help or coercion. But what if...?

"What were you going to tell me?" Layla interrupted, hurling the White mystery to the back of my brain.

I blinked rapidly, my stomach dropping at the warning in her eyes. "Huh?"

"Mikki said she hopes you finally told me whatever you needed to. So..."

Thanks, Mikki. I wanted to laugh at the screws my old friend put me to, but Layla started worrying herself into a pretzel. I reached over to her when a hand smacked against the glass of the window beside me. One of my neighbors, the man with a stark white forehead and red cheeks, screamed that we needed to either keep driving or park the vehicle.

Startled and chastised, we both leaped out of the car. Layla dashed around the front, away from the nosy neighbor stalking back inside his house. He'd probably sit at the picture window, waiting for a squirrel he could scream at to wander on his lawn. I froze by the side of the road, staring at the tamped-down tire marks in the remaining snow. Layla's escape paused her almost within arm's reach.

"You…" She slipped in her shoes, reminding me that I needed to get inside soon and find a real pair. "You don't have to tell me. It's fine. I can—"

I caught her hand, pulling Layla over the snow into my embrace. A cute blush traced over her forehead, which called to my lips. I brushed my nose against the puff of her hair and breathed deep. The lightning was soft, calm, distant, but always ready to spark.

"I've been trying to tell you, for a while now that…" Why was this so hard?

Witch, werewolves, demons, hunters, nymphs. Pick any one of those problems, then add nursing school on top like a stress cherry.

But Layla rustled her fingers back through my hair, soothing away the lump in the hated blond locks. "Cal—"

"I love you."

Her eyes opened wide and my mind fully blanked. I needed to say more. I should elaborate. Tell her she was the first person I ever wanted to stay for. The only one I trusted outside my real family. The woman I wanted to wake beside and let steal all my best flannel shirts. Even if she was a witch, even if I was a wolf, even if the world hated both of us. I needed to want her and wanted to need her.

"Uh..." I began, and a giggle swept over her beautiful face.

"I love you too," she said, straining on her toes to reach me. I caught her and lifted her higher, meeting Layla's sweet and wonderful lips for a kiss that ignited such a heat that the snow melted from my feet. There was a bedroom just across the street with a bed that needed two bodies to warm up the sheets. I slipped my tongue in her mouth, hoping to inspire Layla with my same thoughts.

"Woo!"

We sprang apart and whipped our heads around. With hands cupped around her mouth, Dana shouted from across the street, "Fucking finally!"

"Oh god," Layla muttered, her head dropping. The fine blush on her cheeks was a raging volcano on mine. "What are you doing here?" she shouted to our friend.

"You mean aside from catching you two sucking face? How long has this been going on? And you ain't said a word," Dana bellowed. With no chance of escape, Layla and I walked across the street to join her right outside the gate to my house.

"Things have been...a little crazy lately," Layla said with the shortest but most accurate summation. "But that doesn't answer my question."

"What do you think, Layls?" Dana twisted around her gerontology book and smacked it for emphasis.

"Back to the grind," Layla said, tipping her head to the pile of studying ahead of us. She turned to me, her smile strained but patient.

"Here," I said, pressing my key into her hand. "You guys head on in and set up. I'll get our stuff from the car. And…" Leaning closer, I brushed my lips against her ear to whisper, "You can keep it."

Layla snickered in shock at what I gave her, then wrapped her arm with Dana's. The two marched through the gate for the front door. When I had first come back to the city, this had been a stop. A means to an end. I'd needed a house with walls to hide what I was. To disguise myself from the pack.

Now, I had a home and someone worth finding inside.

Chapter Twenty-One

A lone coyote paused above the desert dunes, a scent catching its attention. The long run back to its den was forgotten, the hungry animal sniffing beside the smoking remnants of human matter. Trash could be a source of food, but even the coyote knew better than to draw too close to that hunk of scrap metal in its desert.

The scent grew stronger, directing it farther from the scrap statue. Its tiny paws dashed over virgin sand, the marks long hidden by ever-temperamental winds. But the coyote knew something lurked under the waves. Tipping its nose down, it began to dig.

Fingers shattered from the ground, red sand sluicing from the nails piercing to the sky. The coyote shrieked, the stench of human overpowering its nose. It dashed for a rock, no longer watching as the sands parted like a massive hole opened up around the hand.

Grunting and snarling, the palm managed to grab onto a dying root. An entire arm appeared below the desert stars, then a head shielded by a mask of black.

When the second arm emerged, the free hand ripped the mask away.

Detective Eve gasped in the fresh air, her eyes swollen and red from the million micro-cuts of burned sand turned to glass. The pain meant nothing as long she could breathe. Only oxygen mattered, her lungs filling with pure air instead of the recycled options the mask afforded her.

Every breath refreshed her body. She stood on shaky legs, her foot planted on the sign ripped from the side of their van. Most of the sand covered it, leaving only the letters *mal Con* visible.

Shaking out her hair, Eve didn't stare at the smashed van, or cast a single glance at the dead men inside. No, she pulled out her phone to find it cracked but functioning.

A smile burned on her face. There were the pictures of not only the nymph they'd missed, but the witch as well. Pressing the single Call button, she began to walk out of the desert.

"Detective Stone?" Eve's words echoed across the indigo night, a full moon bearing witness. "You'll want to see this."

Want to see more from this author?
Here's a taster for you to enjoy!

Coven of Desire: Whisper
Ellen Mint

Excerpt

A cross march wind seared through the air and straight up my skirt. I latched onto the hemline and stumbled. The back of my ankle twisted, causing the side of my foot to touch the frozen, drink-splattered cement. Disgust crawled up my spine from who knew what was sprayed outside the club buzzing with college students about to flee town on spring break. I tried to contort my body to both gain my balance, yank my foot off the ground, and somehow keep my foot as far from me as possible.

The neon lights of a dancing horse outside the Gallon Stallion blurred into warp lines. That vomit and urine soaked ground I'd tried to avoid rushed up to meet me. I foresaw a broken nose in my future. Hands unnaturally warm in this unforgiving night's chill wrapped around my waist.

I didn't just stop falling, I righted onto my stilettos while blinking in surprise. The hands became arms winding around me and a hot breath curled around my ear. "Beware the terrain, there is treachery in the air."

My skin shivered from the heat of his body caressing mine. March's unforgiving cold tried to break in between us but he rarely left any room. Shaking my head, I tried to fight off the sexual hunger of my personal incubus. It was like attempting to battle a ten-story lizard with a french fry.

Falling into a warm, clean bed with Ink brushing his fingertips over every inch of my skin sounded better with every frost-tipped breath. Heat finally wound its way down my thighs, and I turned to face him…when a car turned and slowed.

Jet black, the Mustang was a few decades out of date but kept in great condition. It shined like an oil river as it stopped right beside me. The dancing neon horse galloped on the hood while the driver rolled down his window. A face eclipsed by shadow called out, "Layla Leeland?"

"That's me," I said, my heart racing. Was this one it? I glanced back at my partner in more than one sense.

While I was freezing in my dress that was too tight thanks to lots of studying pizza nights, Ink showed no signs of the cold. He'd dressed in his usual crimson shirt and black slacks, but left the top three buttons undone. On his shirt. Not that it'd take much to get his pants opened.

As I leaned closer to Ink, the driver suddenly called out, "I only take one passenger!"

I nodded hard to my incubus. He clasped his hands around mine and tugged me closer to whisper. "Are you certain?"

Only one way to know. Taking my purse from Ink, I said to the driver, "No problem." To Ink I added, "I'm certain you can find your own way."

"I have been known to improvise a time or two." His wavy black hair caught in the wind, aiding in the nonchalant air projecting off him. But in his eyes, fire flickered against the amber irises.

With a set in my shoulders, I opened the backdoor of the Mustang. Water dribbled from the upholstery, drops striking the dry blacktop. I slipped into the car and closed the door. It surprised me to find dry leather caught my nearly-exposed ass, but I was grateful to be out of the cold.

The Mustang roared to life. With the edge of my vision, I watched Ink pass by. For a moment black wings of shadow trailed behind him.

Stop worrying, Layla. You've been through worse. Standing outside clubs until two in the morning for starters. I rubbed my legs to try to get some life back.

"Any chance you could turn the heat on back here?" I asked.

"Sorry, lass. Heater doesn't work," the driver called. In the rearview mirror, I could only see the lip of a cap tugged tight over his eyes. The rest of his face hugged the shadows even as streetlights buzzed past. "You use DriveDrop a lot?"

I checked my phone. The screen was fully cracked not from attacking witch hunters or even werewolf claws, but my keys rattling around in the same pocket. A dozen other ride share apps were open, all waiting for pickup. I quickly closed each one while smiling. "No. This is my first time."

"Good. Good. You go to university?"

His accent flitted in and out like a brush fire he couldn't quite stamp down. I moved to put my phone in my purse when a text message popped up from Calvin. He was worried. "Huh? Uh, yeah. I'm a nursing student."

"Oh, so you like saving people?"

"As many as I can." There wasn't time to soothe my beast boyfriend. Slipping the phone into my purse, I glanced out the windows. I hadn't been this far downtown in months, maybe years. In my younger days, I'd have thought nothing of staying up 'til two, four, even six in the morning.

God, I sounded like a decrepit crone at twenty-five.

A hair caught against my neck and I absently moved to scratch it, when the driver's head snapped up. In an instant, I remembered what was hidden under my full hair and dropped my hands to my lap. Nothing pierced the shadows of his face but a tongue. Wet and slathering, the driver drew it across his open lips. They didn't move as he asked, "You from here? Got a lot of family."

The only family I knew of was six feet under in a random cemetery. I wound up in this city because it was where my life stopped thanks to a reckless driver. Biting my lip to keep the roiling thoughts at bay, I glanced up at the shadows in the mirror. "No."

Only the salivating tongue lashed through the air as an answer. A force rocketed me up out of my seat, the wheels striking something hard. It sent my purse tumbling, and the edge of my book poked from the folds. My spell book. Shit.

I raced to cram it back in to try and hide it. The hairs on the back of my neck rose. Piercing through the shadows of the drawn hat, the driver's eyes focused on me. Did he see the proof I was a witch?

A low chuckle rose, his laugh matching the rumbling of the road under the tires. When did the car speed up? The city's streetlights were a myopic blur. Instinctively, I locked my hand around my purse and held my breath.

"Wh...?" *The architecture's all wrong.* My brain screamed that fact at me as I stared up not at the seventies cement apartment buildings that made up my neighborhood but warehouses. The driver rammed the

Mustang up a ramp. It sent me flying skyward again. "Where are we?"

"Packing district, I think. Lots of unloading and the like. Not an easy place to find," the driver said.

Only the stretch of the half-moon reached through the cold March sky. The city lights faded to a blotchy gray behind us. A pounding began in my heart, one I'd come to recognize as my innate warning system. I had to get out of here. This was stupid. What was I thinking? I'm not ready to…

The car swung a turn and ahead of us rested the choppy, endless depths of blackest ink. A single buoy cast a red light from the tip, revealing the rolling waves of the great lake we were driving straight for. "What are you doing?" I shrieked, clamping onto my purse.

His laugh shifted into an unholy whinny. The engine roared, shooting us at fifty miles-an-hour up a pile of pallets. They crunched under the wheels like the bones of children in a cauldron. I gritted my teeth, my soul wrenching at the sound. A steel barrier wrapped around the dock, trying to keep the lake life away from dry land.

It didn't even give the madman pause. Giggling in glee, he rammed straight into the barrier. The iron ripped in half as we flew into the air. I lashed a hand out to try and catch myself. The palm planted onto the back of his seat, my nails digging into the headrest, when the whole car splattered into the freezing water.

"What the fuck are you doing?" I screamed and reached for the door handle. I heard the sound of the car being put into park, as if it mattered while sank into the lake. Water seeped up through the floorboards, its icy grip stabbing into my bare toes. I tried to pull away, when I realized my feet were trapped. The soles of my shoes were glued to the floor. Every time I tugged, nothing happened. Not even the carpet would come up.

"Sit back, don't struggle," the madman said calmly.

No fucking way was I going to let him drown me. I moved to yank my foot out of my shoe when I realized the hand on his headrest was glued down too. An unnerving warmth pulsed against it, like a heartbeat inside a whale.

With only one hand left to me, I wrapped it around my wrist and tried to pull. All it got me was a slow laugh from the maniac. "I got a bad feeling about you. If'n we'd met in person, I'd ha'e sensed it. Technology. The great equalizer, eh?" He waved his phone in the rearview — which was when I realized the mirror dripped green slime. My reflection faded to a bubbling mass of mucus.

"Oh, god!" Water washed up to my knees. My skin ached from the bursting of goosebumps, but I couldn't do anything. My legs were trapped, my hand stuck, and freezing cold water was going to drown me.

"Told ya not to fight it. Makes the meat all tough." He smiled, this time revealing his teeth below the hat. They were serrated like a shark's. "Just let it go. Sit back and wait for the inevitable."

"Fuck you!" I shouted and reached for my purse. Damn it. It too was glued to the sinking car. Water seeped up over the seat, waves rushing into my purse. I didn't care about my phone, but focused on the only means of escape — my book.

"Whatcha doing there?"

"Ending you." It wasn't that great of a line, rendered toothless as the car buckled to the right. My book tumbled from my bag, the front page suckered to the gooey seat. Now I could feel the tendrils of the creature suckering to the whole of my back. Why did I wear a backless dress?

Straining, I tried to reach for my book even with my hand and feet trapped. The creature laughed, all semblance of his human shell fading away. A full whinny, high-pitched and squealing like nails on a chalkboard, erupted from the monster.

"What are you up to now, witch?"

What was I? I needed my book. It was the only way to… Water swept up my chest, the cold punching into me harder than a fist to my ribs. All breath fled my lungs in an instant and I blanched. Hold it. Hold it for as long as possible.

Sucking in air, I glared at the creature taunting me. It'd reformed to nothing more than a swiveling pillar of green goo, but that jaunty newsboy cap remained. "Do not fight the inevitable."

"Why are you doing this?" I shouted, as if knowing why the monster wanted to kill me would help stop it.

The green blob split apart and elongated to that of a horse's mouth. It opened wider, drawing me to the razor teeth bursting from inside. "To survive. You humans have such delectable organs. It's cruel of you to keep them all to yourself."

"I think my liver's quite happy where it is," I said, only for water to rush into my mouth. Straining, I tried to tip my head back, but it sent more waves up my nose. A choke burst from my lungs, spraying the swallowed lake water at the monster.

It shook its deformed horse head but didn't let me go. Why couldn't all these damn creatures die from the common cold? Not about to give up, I tugged on my seat one last time. But there was no escape.

Tipping my head back, I pulled in the last of the air I could and sunk under. Sound dulled, the beating of my panicking heart overtaking me. I'd hoped once under he'd let go, or his glue would dissolve, but no luck.

"Abandon your struggles, witch," the creature taunted. His words didn't slip from the horse's mouth now submerged, but reverberated up my nerves attached to the seat and into my brain. "The water will cascade down your lungs and I shall feast on your corpse."

No!

Home of Erotic Romance

Sign up for our newsletter and find out about all our romance book releases, eBook sales and promotions, sneak peeks and FREE romance books!

About the Author

Ellen Mint adores the adorkable heroes who charm with their shy smiles and heroines that pack a punch. She recently won the Top Ten Handmaid's Challenge on Wattpad where hers was chosen by Margaret Atwood. Her books, Undercover Siren and Fever are available at Amazon as well as a short story in the Lucky Between The Sheets anthology. Married, she lives in Nebraska with her dog named after Granny Weatherwax. Her hobbies include gaming, painting, and halloween prop making. The basement is full of skeletons because they ran out of room in the closets.

Ellen loves to hear from readers. You can find her contact information, website details and author profile page at https://www.totallybound.com